A Road You Don't want To Travel

Captain David Belding

Copyright 2023 by Captain David Belding

ISBN: 979-8-9881416-0-0 (Softcover)
ISBN: 979-8-9881416-1-7 (eBook)

Library of Congress Control Number: 2023911499

All right reserved No part of this book may be reproduced or transmitted in any form or any means, electronic or mechanical, including photocopying, recording, or by any information storage and retrieval system, without permission in writing from the copyright owner.

E-mail: belding.david49@Gmail.com

Crown 888 Press

Index

Introduction
1 Where is this
2 Meanwhile 2 miles away
3 It came from the sky
4 That smell funny
5 The Plan
6 The Alien Come Again
7 Another Compound
8 While in A Control Center
9 what to do with a stranger
10 A can of Peaches
11 Cameras everywhere
12 The Doors
13 Getting everyone together
14 Camp three again
15 The takeover
16 News is out
17 Ted Donaldson
18 What the Government
19 Welcome to 21
20 So this is what they eat
21 A New Town
22 NewsMan Ted Donaldson
23 The Court settlement
24 Met your Guardian Angel
25 He's is Not Guilty
26 Krima
27 Lema
28 It Was Kidnapping
29 Lorla
30 Bus/Motor home
31 The Fire
32 Missing Guardian Angel
33 BOLO
34 A short Story
35 Nancy
36 Oil
37 Sink or Swim
38 A Goodwill Mission
39 The Earthquake
40 Ammie
41 Buddy

INTRODUCTION

These stories are work of fiction, name, characters, places and incidents either are the product of author's imagination or are used fictitiously, and any resemblance to any accrual persons living or dead, events or local is entirely coincidental. HOWEVER there are three stories that if you take out the Guardian Angels really happen and are the basis of the stories. With some of the circumstance in the stories, you would think that it was actually a Guardian Angel giving guidance.

CHAPTER 1

Where Is This ALocla

It was a stormy night, the wipers were barley keeping up I looked in the side mirror and there were two shinning eyes looking back at me I turned my head and look closer. Nothing there, looking again in the mirror nothing there either. Probably a Volkswagen, being the super trucker he was only 60,000 sixty thousand pounds on the road, he wasn't about to be passed by something that small, as the highway changed from four lanes to two lanes. Either that or he must be getting tired only on the road for three hours after the mandatory ten hours off. Maybe it was the rain that was stopping; he could see most of the road ahead but not the surrounding hills. The road became bumper. Then smoothed out and then into sand, must have been the rain had wash down on the road. No something was wrong the rain had quite and he was driving in a desert, must have taken the wrong road in the rain. Looking around there was no way to turn around the truck with a fifty three foot trailer without getting stuck and I did not want to stop, looking in the mirror how far back was the black top road? But instead of a road behind there was those eyes again.

He step down on the pedal and the eyes got further back till they were just small spots then disappeared behind him. By now he was quite, always down the dirt road. When he spotted something lying by the road, as he came closer he could see it was a body. He locked up the breaks and almost hit it. He jumped from the cab and went to the body turning it over; he discovered it was a half-naked lady. He took off his jacket and covered her up. She spoke in a language he did not understand, but motioned that she wanted water or something to eat from the look of her he was sure that it was water. Going to his truck he retrieved the gallon bottle of water that was only half full. Taken it to her she looked at it strangely. Till he shows her the water, then she started drinking it down. Finally he took it away from her then told her to slow down then handed it back. Finally she put down the water, looked around till she spotted the truck and move back pointing saying something that sounded like (monster).

No this truck is no monster as he went over and patted the finder. Just a minuet as he held up his hand. Then he went to the back of the trailer and taken out a case of peaches. There was forty thousand pounds of them in the back. He would have to pay for one case if he could figure a way out of this nightmare but they should understand it was going to a good cause, he put the case in the truck and took out one can. Good he thought it had a pop top on it like you see on a coke can. Then took out his pocket knife he offered half. She pushed it, away so he ate one, then pulled out another one and handed it to her. Carefully she took a small bite, and then reached for the rest taken the whole half. Then looking up at him as he dug out another half soon the whole can was gone. He got another can opened it Peaches he said. Peaches she said holding out her hand. Close enough, he said as he handed her the can.

Pointing at himself I'm David, pointing at her you are? Pointing at her

I'm David. No I'm David you are?

She got the ideal then. I'm Alcola pointing to herself. Where do you live? Where do you live she repeated. No I live in truck pointing at himself then at the truck. Truck, she repeated I live Como. David hoped that meant in the city of Como but the way she pointed it meant far away. David stepped off the road it was still too soft to drive the truck on other than the road.

David turned to Alcola helping her up then headed toward the truck, she pull back KETO. No keto he said patting the fender come see we go to Como. She followed him to the door when he open it she shook her head, JA PO TATED. It is OK come, come, he motion her in with his hands. Then he stepped up into the truck and held out his hand. She took it and followed him. When they were both in the truck David slid behind the steering wheel and started the motor when he did, Alcola started beating on the window trying to get out. He tapped her on leg, it's OK, it's OK he repeated we go to Como. She looked closely in to his eyes and saw that he was not going to harm her and set back. David put the truck in gear and they were going, he was still not sure where but within the hour he saw a group of people standing in front of a large cave, kids were running toward the parents who were holding spears and bows with Arrows, with stone tips these are primitive people David thought, as he stopped the truck and turned the engine off he reached across and opened the door on the passenger side and let Alcola out.

CHAPTER 2

Meanwhile 2 miles away

What the hell is that?
    It's a truck.
    I know it's a truck! How did it get into A two Billion dollar government's top secret secured experimental area?
It just drove in.
How did it know where to go?
Well it picked up SPC 127 at the edge of the boundary.
How in the hell did she get to the edge of the boundary?
We flew her there.
What the hell do you mean we flew her there? What the hell is going on?
We must have picked up her son from section 1 and she held on to the tricoptor and she was a strong one, held on till we got to the boundary. Then she fell off. She fell fifty feet and she should be dead. That's what we figured so we left her there, to be picked up later. But before we could get back the truck showed up and she wasn't dead. So she must have told him where to go
And when the SAM HELL were you going to tell me about this? What I'm seeing on this video is twenty four years of study just gone to shit.
Well sir you were at the convention and as we decide to and see how someone from an advance civilization would react to the tribe.

Who the hell are we, what kind of idiots I'm working with?

The ground supervisor and I said one of the scientist said looking at the ground.

Shaking his head then he looked up at the video, what is this? a truck full of food?

We didn't know the food was in there it had cans of peaches. The poor scientist said sinking back in his chair.

Well pick him up when he is away from everyone else, you Moreno's.

CHAPTER 3

It Came From the Sky

After a week with the tribe, they were getting used to David being around. David had almost given up hope someone would find him. When something went crazy, from out of the sky came an airplane like ship. It hovered about a hundred feet above the community the children ran and the men thru spears and shot arrows that seemed to bounce off a protective shield around the plane. Then thing really got crazy, a beam came out from the bottom and scanned around till it came on a small boy and the next thing David saw was the boy was be raising into the plane, then returned and scanned till it found another child this time a young girl and again she was floated into the plane. After the bean had collected three kids it shot straight up till it disappeared into the sky. This gave David the ideal that it wasn't just a plane but a space ship. He was just standing there in amassment the whole seen had only taken about ten minutes. What the hell just happen? He asked.

We don't know, it has been happening every full moon. Last time they took my son and I held on to his lag till I could hold on any more that is how I end up in the waste land where you found me in your strange machine at first I thought you were with them.

Grub the leader of the tribe came over and informed David that this had started a long time ago and there was nothing they could do and the kids have never been seen again. There is really not anything we can do about it. Our weapons are useless against it

David was still wondering what had just happen. He had never heard of this happen other than on TV, where a space ship comes down and lights comes out and abducts people. He did notice that the spears and arrows would just bounce off the shield but when the beam was searching and picking up kids that some of the arrows would hit the ship. This started David's mind working. Suppose that when they used their lift up beam or whatever it was, that somehow they could shoot something up then and put the beam out of commission. He didn't think the gun in his truck would do it, it was only a 22. He was going to need something bigger. And that was when he set mind on finding some way of stop this abducting.

After several days of think about it, He was going to need a canon but their soft metal they were making their spears and arrow tips out of, would not do. Then one day looking at his truck, he thought of the drive line hell the truck wasn't going anywhere any ways. So he got out the few tools he did have and removed the drive line and took it over the men working with metal and explains to them with the help of Alcola, what he wanted. Now he needed to figure out a way to fire it. Oh well it was something to do, till he figured out a way out of where ever he was. The one can of starting fluid was not going to be enough but that was all he had.

A few days later while think over this problem David thoughts were interrupted with several of the children came in chattering about how men had taken three of the other children. David had not seen the space ship so he asked Alcola.

It seemed that some members from a tribe over the other side of the hill had come over and kidnaped some of their kids.

What the hell is with this taken of kids around here David asked?

My guess is they are going to use our kids for the next time the flying craft comes.

Well that not going to happen, let's go get them back.

That is not wise they are a lot bigger tribe, and they were mostly men and we have mostly Women. There is no way we cannot win a fight against them, just let it go.

I'll be damn; I'm going to go get them back. Can you show me where they have taken them?

Yes I will go with you, we shell die together.

We are not going to die; we are just going to ask them to give them back.

That is really not a good ideal, Alcola said, but if you have your mind set on it and I cannot stop you we had better leave now.

One minute I need something out of the truck. As David headed to the truck and got his 22 from under the seat and stuck it in his belt. Then grab a case of peaches to do some bargain with. Then headed over to Alcola, ok let's go. As they headed over the hill that was more like a mountain David decided after an hour of walking. That case of peaches that was fifteen pounds had turned into one hundred pounds in David's mind and he was wondering if it was worth bringing it. When they reach the summit and started down.

It was just about dark when they came to the other tribe's compound this one was different than Alcola's instead of caves they lived in two large lodges. Alcola warned David that it was a dangerous ideal. He ignores the warning and walk straight into the camp like he own the place.

Three of the men came out to meet them. The other people just step aside when the men came out one the size of Grub David could see he was the leader

OK you must be the leader who is your second in command if something should happen to you.

I am Griz and this is Orka here next to me as Griz pointed to the man on the right.

Alright David pulled out his gun and shot Orka in the lag dropping him to the ground. David put the gun back in his belt, then walked over to the man on the left of Griz and handed him the case of peaches here these are good to eat taking out a can of peaches and popping it open thinking glad it had the finger opening ring. Taking one half out and eating it then handing the can to Griz took one still looking at the gun in David belt. We will be taken the three children back with us when we leave.

Yes but you must not leave till morning. We will welcome you tonight it is very dangerous on the trail in the dark. You will be safe here you have my word on that; this was said by Griz now we will eat he said as he walked away.

This was all translated to David by Alcola

Can we trust him David asked?

Yes a leader only hold control by his word. Which means you did it, we will leave tomorrow.

Well in that case let's eat. I would like to talk with this Griz and mostly I'll need you to translate.

At the main lodge Griz motion David over next to him. There was only one empty chair at that end of the table. Dave grabbing Alcola hand and took her with him and set her in the empty chair pulling it out then pushing it back in after she sat down then standing behind her, looking around.

Griz watched this, then motion with his hand for the member on the other side for the man to move and in the same motion waved to David to sit there saying something Dave did not understand.

He says you have big hands, Alcola translated.

David just smiled he didn't think that is exactly what he said. After dinner David asked Alcola to translate she nodded, and then David turned his chair toward Griz. I have plan for stopping the flying machine but it can only be done if both tribes fight together would he be interested After Alcola translated Griz looked and nodded. David explain his ideal of stopping the space ship by showing him his gun then demonstrated how he would be using a much bigger one Griz seem to smile and nodded again.

David had notice a young man sitting in the back trying to avoid attrition and David had seen him before only it was over in Alcola camp that gave him another ideal. Say Griz you have a lot of men over here and they have a lot of woman at Alcola camp what would think of sending a few men over to Alcola camp and see if they are looking for a mate.

Griz nodded his head and said something that Alcola translated that he agreed and it was a good ideal.

They slept that night without any trouble; but David had slept very lightly making sure nothing did.

CHAPTER 4

That Smells Funny

On the way back to Como the village where Alcola lived. Along with the missing kids and five young men, one he had seen over there before and he had made sure that he was in the group.

They came on a place in the trail. That smelled like rotten eggs he had not notice before. Alcola put her hand over her nose and mouth turned to him and said smell very bad.

David had smell that smell before but could not place it. So he told everyone to take a break while he went to investigate. He walked to the top of the hill and the minute he saw the yellow sulfur it all came back to him. What the smell was. As he turned around and headed back to the people waiting for him he was forming a plan. He was remembering a long time back, when he would make a spoke gun using a spoke from a bicycle and matches head made of sulfur. The rest of the way to Como he was forming a plan in his head. He was so engrossed in the plan; he didn't even know they had walked into the village. Until everyone came running out, the woman running to the children and the men with weapons.

When he realized what was happen, he step forward and held up both hands and yelled Quinta(which he had learned in their language meant stop). The men stopped the woman keep coming and grab their kids. David tried to explain that there was no more war with the other camp. But not being that familiar with the language it was not coming out right. So Alcola stepped forward and explained that both tribes would be getting along. And that they would be working together to stop the mystery ship from taken their kids.

After a few seconds the men accepted the ideal and welcome the five strangers into their group. After Alcola explained to David what she had said. He wasn't sure he really had a plan. It was still in his head, and that he just felt his duty to do something to stop the kidnapping and it calms everyone down so he just went along with it.

CHAPTER 5

The Plan

The plan called for a weapon that would be more powerful than what the aliens had seen so far. Up till now they only had to deal with arrows and spears. He did have his gun but only a few bullets and he really wanted to save them.

He had thought of the canon using the ether but now with the use of sulfur. He could make it more powerful or even a bomb. Whoever they were, He did know of their week point. When they open the doors to use their beam or whatever that force to life a body off the ground and into their space craft. The Problem would be getting the bomb into the craft before the beam has the kid inside so the timing had to be just right or the bomb might kill the boy or girl which it ever they decided to take.

He went to see how they were doing with cutting the drive line from the truck and the old hack saw with only two extra blades. He had shown then that they had to heat it up to make the metal soft, Sort of take the temper out of one end. They were about half thru it but they had beat it with rocks and it was more oblong instead of round. The good part is they had only used one blade. He replaces the blade and explained not to use the rocks it will not break off. They had to cut it all the way thru.

Several weeks later the canon was almost ready. He had gone with Alcola and a basket back to the sulfur field and had brought back about two pounds of sulfur. He had taken the saw and cut a hole just enough to make a small hole in the other to be used to set off the ether that would set off the sulfur. That was the plan he hope it would work and not blow up killing everyone. Next he had to make a bomb and a way to set it off.

What did he have in or on the truck he could use, he was sure the truck would never move again he had showed them how to use thing off the truck to put on the end of their arrows to make them more deadly. It had come in handy when the wort hog had come in to camp and they killed it. They had meat for a week. I don't think that their pointed stick would have killed it before it kills a few of them.

Now back to the problem the bomb. He found a box full of miscellaneous nuts, bolts, screws, but no way to make it in to a bomb. He knew they had clay pot. But would they hold together? How would he set it off if it did hold together? DUCK TAPE it is the answer to everything and being a good trucker he had a roll in the truck, if he could find it?

He went and found Alcola and told her his plan and asked her to make him two clay pots but not like regular pots these would be, he held up his hand showing her about six inches long each and smaller than to inside of the driveline and to put the nuts, bolts and screw into the clay, She question it but agreed. A week later she showed him what he ask for. While she was making the pots he was experimenting with some sulfur and diesel from the truck. It was defiantly flammable. Now for a fuse he took one of his most valuable bullets apart to get to the gun powder and tread from a rag he had in the truck and rolled it together he figured it should be about a foot long. To his dismay it took the powder from three bullets to get it right. But at the end he was satisfied.

Now to set it up lay it on rocks and aiming it right. The kids would go to a mark spot that they had marked off; the canon was aimed above them to about twenty-five in the air. If all went as last time this just might work but he had some doubts there could be so many thing that could wrong.

OK all was ready now nothing more to do, but to just wait that was the hard part. One day it rained and the end of the canon had to be covered up. He hoped that they caught it in time; if the sulfur got wet it would not work.

CHAPTER 6

THE ALIENS COME AGAIN

Everything was ready when the aliens came again they would be in for a surprise. The waiting was hard and soon it was almost forgotten. Life had gone back to normal except for the part of the men from over the hill and several of the women had gone over there. Both tribes were getting along.

Out of nowhere the alarm went off the aliens were coming. It was few months later so no one was prepared the kid had forgot the spot to stand, Alcola was running around trying to get the kids to the right spot David was getting the canon ready. Hue was trying to get the fire stick over to him and it went out twice finely he had it. Everything was ready, but the space craft stop in a different place and the beam was coming out in an angle. It was like the aliens know what was happen and they were ready for it.

David pick up the fuse and shove it in the cannon and picking up the cannon and aiming it at the open door in the craft. Shouted at Hue to light it, there was a hesitation then the cannon fired. His aim was good one boy was half way to the door in the beam. The bomb beat him in and when the boy was just about in, the bomb went off. With such a blast it surprise even David. The boy fell to the ground breaking his lag. But the space craft try pulling away only going a little way till it fell to the ground. Two men in white coats came out. Follow by two men in blue uniforms holding some kind of guns. It fired a blast that didn't hurt anyone but blinded every one for a few minutes when everyone could see all four people had disappeared.

David went over to where the boy who had almost been kidnap and was laying on the ground with a broken lag. The people had gather around the mother was holding the boy. David had everyone stand back, and then pointed at the two of the biggest men. You two come over here and hold him down as he grab the boy's foot. Do not worry, it will be alright this might hurt a little, ok on three ready. The boy with tears in his eyes nodded. One, two, he never got to three with a quick jerk he pulled on the foot setting it back in place. The boy gave a sharp yell. Still holding the foot he called Alcola over. Go get me two stick about this long. Still holding the foot and with the other hand measured about half way up the boy's thigh. And about this big around making a sign with his fingers the size of a silver dollar, and some leather, strapping. After setting the make shift splint he step back telling the mother keep him off it four sunrises then only little movements for three full moons and it should be alright. I hope he said to himself.

Alcola came up to him, you are really an amazing person, then she screamed what happen to your arms he look down at his arms were burned fairly bad.

It's not as bad as it looks the canon was hot when I had to move it so it would be in the right spot.

Come over here and sit down, you are not the only healer around as she ran into the cave and came back with some aloe Vera leaves Dave did recognize them , she broke them open then and rub the sap on his arms. It did take the pain out of the burns. That he had not notice till she mentions it, he leaned over and kissed her whisper in her ear you are a great healer too.

Around an hour later another space craft show up and hover over the down space craft and using the same kind of beam pick up the pieces of the down craft then flew away to the north.

David stuck around for a few weeks, but couldn't help of thinking about the space craft and the four supposing space man.

A Road You Don't Want to Travel

Epically the way they disappeared so fast and how it only took fifteen minutes for the second craft to show up. The strangest part was they look human and he wasn't sure but he thought the men in white coats spoke in a language he recognized. The blinding light that came out of their guns didn't hurt and one just temporary blinded everyone.

CHAPTER 7

Another Compound

David waited a few days then told Alcola that he was going for a walk and most likely would be gone for a few days. Ok I will get my pack and some food.

No not this time I need to do this alone, don't worry I will be back. With that he kissed her and headed off south then a half hour later he headed north going around the camp.

It was getting toward night fall; he had no idea how far he had gone. So David started to set up camp and to build a small fire in case one of those wild hogs shows up. But when he pulled a branch down, He found a wire fence behind it. Looking left and right it ran as far as he could see, then he looked up and spotted the cameras running both ways. He jumped back to the woods to study it better without being seen. He studies the situation. It looked good that he had step out between the two cameras and may not have been seen.

David spent the night thinking about the fence. When he did drift off and sleep he dreamed of going under lying face down and carrying a rifle it was more like a musket with only one shot. Then the dream would switch to going under the fence with his back on the ground carrying a more modern rifle with many shots. Once that night he had the feeling someone was watching him and turning fast got a quick glance of the two light before they disappeared The next morning he snicks up to study the fence, in a spot he hope no one could see him. It was at least ten feet tall and ran along as he could see now that he knew what it look like in all of its camouflage. That when he saw something hanging on the fence that made him jumped back it was a sign in English, saying,

DANGER HI VOLTAGE 6000 VOLTS.

David set back in the brush and studies the fence. He knew what to look for he had seen this before and there it was on the other side of the fence about two foot off the ground was the thin wire on insulators and another wire running along the top that he had not notice before. He had touched the main fence before and knew it was not hot, so he started finding a way thru it or under it.

He went to the spot here the camas were pointing both ways and with a stick started to dig. The fence only went down a few inches in the ground. After an hour he had a hole under the fence he could lay on his back and slide under all the time looking out for the hot wire. He wasn't sure if it was really hot with 6,000 volts but he was not going to take a chance. Once on the other side he places bushes over the hole so no one would notice.

David kept on his walk about still going north; keep an eye open for whatever the fence was built for. Coming around a large rock he came face to face not a freest wild boar but a young man with a bow and arrow that axially had a head in it made of metal.

Pointing his arrow toward David he asked in the language that Dave was just learning. I'm David from the camp of Como. I just got here.

Come with me as he waved his arrow in the direction he had just come from.

David started the way he had come, a few more young men joined behind them. When in camp it seemed a step forward in time, there were individual huts. He was taken to the village when a young girl came running out saying something he didn't understand.

The boys all raised their bows and spears with the metal tips. David raised his hands and asked what did she say?

She said you came in large thing that moves but does not go up in sky and you know Alcola.

That right and I came looking for the missing kids. Are you one of them?

Yes I have been here more than anyone. My name is Washen but you have more suns than I so how did you get here. You say that you come from Como? How did you get here?

I walked it took two suns.

Our mother and father come from Como and Ubec you can get us back there?

David had not heard the name of the other camp where Griz Lived. Yes but I think someone does not want that to happen and they will try to stop us and they are watching us all the time so we will have to be careful and have a good plan. Do you know if Alcola son is here?

I will ask here you sit and eat.

David sat down and one of the women brought some meat and something that look like a potato. Do you hunt the wild boar here he asked.

No we don't have them, here we have *kehav* here. They are harder to catch but better to eat and more of them.

CHAPTER 8

Meanwhile in a Control Center

Looking at the screen WHAT THE FUCK just happen?
The man just shot one of the antelope.
I know the man just shot an antelope, HOW IN THE HELL did he get in there.
I believe it is the man who drove into camp one with the truck.
What the hell is going on first he's in camp one with a truck, now he is in camp three with a gun? Go out and pick him up now.
We did say he has a gun, you saw what he did with a canon.
Well he doesn't have a canon now, just a damn gun now go get him out of there. You have him in here when I get back in a week I have a meeting with Senator Rieinigton. And don't let him screw up anything else, do I make myself clear.
David saw the Vertma too late; there were three men in white coats, already on the ground with guns, they seem to appear out of some cave in the rocks but he did not notice it before as the dart hit him. He only had time to duck behind the rocks, and hide his gun under a rock when everything went blank.
When he came awake, he was in a room. With two men wear suits,(Who are you and how did you get into a government high secured compound)?

Frist of all where the hell is here this, seem like some kind of twilight zone?

You are in a secured government aria in the middle of an important government experiment. We have taken infants and raised them here to study the evolution of man, without any contact with the outside world; we have been studying them for twenty four years. Then you came along in your fucking truck.

And your gun another man added.

What kind of sick baster's are you, just ripping kids away from their parents.

We didn't take the kids from their parents. They were orphans or baby that their parents had given them up at birth. Some were abortions cases and we brought then here and place them in compound one.

Well that a lot of bull shit David said, I saw you fly in and take the kids.

Those were the older ones we moved them to compound two the second part of the evaluation without waiting a hundred years. They have a better life than they would in the civilized world. We see that they are feed and safe.

Oh well feed they just have to go out and find it.

No we release in compound one the wild boars when they need it, and they have berries and roots. They seem to be getting along better than the real Neanderthal man, did back in their time.

And in compound two David asked?

That the amazing part the kids seem to have a higher IQ they have gone from Neanderthal into the Bronze Age. All in one generation, like I said the IQ is a lot higher.

Ok that enough information the third man stepped in and said. Now how did you get in the compound one and how did you get subject 127 to talk to you it took us ten years to learn some of their language, and how did you get into compound two.

Oh now they are subject not just people. Are you referring to Alcola. The lady you left in the desert to die.

No you pick her up before we could.

More bull shit David thought she had been out there too long and she was half dead dehydrated she had been there a long time. He had seen how fast they had the brought the other Vertma to pick up the one he had shot down with his makeshift cannon. He also figured out that one of the scientists liked what they were doing and like to talk.

OK this is your thing when are you going to let me go and get back to my life of trucking far from this place?

We really don't know till Ben gets back here.

CHAPTER 9

What to do with a Stranger

While they waited for this Ben, David had the run of the place there were a few rooms that they told him to stay from. That just raised David curiosity. So when no one was looking he slipped in and looked around it had around twenty televisions and he could see inside of both compounds and the cameras on the fence and eight computers. That's all he could see till one of the guards caught him and show him the way out of the room.

A week later Ben came back as he walk in, the second person he met was David.

What the hell is he doing here Ben asked?

You said to pick him up, so we did and brought him here

You moron's I didn't say let him run all over the place.

We didn't let him in the computer room Kelly spoke up.

I want all of you in my office. As the three scientist headed toward the office, David followed. Not you Ben said pointing at Dave.

They all went into the office David drifted off to one side just far away to hear what was going on.

Well what are we going to do about this?

Well just turn him loose and tell him not to mention this one of the scientist said.

Are you that stupid we cannot let someone walk around in public knowing this is here with just a promise not to tell? We have to dispose of him that was Ben speaking.

No we are not going to kill a human this came from another scientist.

How about we just scramble his brain and put him back in compound one. He has been here for five months and no one reported him missing.

How do we do that another asked.

Well we could hypnotize him, that way he would think he was there all the time.

Do any of you know how to hypnotize someone Ben asked?

No but I know someone who does he comes out here once in a while I could call him.

But what happen if this clown come out of it and start remembering thing, Ben asked?

Well we could give him a special word and he would be back under our control. Ok it was all agree on have him hypnotize and put him back in compound one.

David moved off to another room. Thinking if they were going to do that he had to find a word of something that bring him out of this hypnotize scream but what? It has to be something that someone in number one compound would say but nowhere else. Truck, cannon, boars, and many more that he was thinking of, nothing came to mind that someone would know. That night as he lying in his bed it came to him CAN OF PEACHES that is something only people in compound one would know and there were some of them left?

CHAPTER 10

A Can of Peaches

Four days later another scientist showed up. One David had never met; they had him go straight into Ben office. After an hour they call David into the office and introduce him. David had figured out that this was the Hypnotist and if the Can of peaches didn't work this was going to be his last day of living in this world and he would spending the rest of his life living back in time of the stone age. So he sat there repeating can of peaches, to himself can of peaches back to normal, can of peaches, back to normal.

David woke up it was morning; he got up and walked into the cave.

Alcola ran over to him, where have you been?

He look at her questionably I slept outside.

I know but where have you been? You were gone so long I thought they had stolen you to.

What do you mean I was here last night?

No you were gone for many suns, did you hit your head as she check his head for any cuts or bumps.

A boy came over with his lag in a splint, see my lag is better he said.

David looked at him, oh that is good, how did that happen?

You don't know Alcola asked? Come into the cave and lay down there is something wrong.

No need to I feel fine David protested.

You go in and lay down I'll bring you something to eat .you rest and everything will be alright.

David follows her into the cave she notice that this was different too; normally he did only what he wanted to. She had him lay down and brought him some boar meat. That he looked at but didn't eat. So she left and came back with a can of peaches.

What is that David asked?

It's a can of peaches, you like them.

David shook his head as someone would do waking up from sleeping.

Alcola jump back are you alright she asked.

I'm now David remembering everything, He laid there thinking was there any camera in the cave? Yes; it was all coming back to him. He looked up at Alcola and whispered at her I'm fine now do not say anything just go along and we need to go for a walk OK He asked? As he started getting up and walk out the cave entrance.

David still looking around like he was confused He walked out by the truck still looking at it in amassment. He went to the side that he saw on the camera. Then he climbs up on the step and looks in the mirror and jump back as in surprise. Then pick up a rock and broke it. Bending down and picking up a piece of the mirror and palm it then walked around to the other side of the truck.

Alcola just follow along. Wondering what was going on and was he still out of it.

On the other side he took out the mirror and catching the sun lite and reflected it on the rocks around the compound. And sure enough it hit on several shinny spots he didn't leave it there long in case someone was watching the television's in the control room.

Alcola watch all this in wonderment and was about to say something.

David turned his back to the camera and looked at her putting his finger on her lips and shaking his head then motions for her to follow him into the brush. Once in and he was sure there were no camera. He quite acting and turned to her, now listen he said. They caught me and did something to my head so I would not remember anything and they can say something and make me not remember anything again and only you can get me back by saying can of peaches do you understand?

She looked at him in bewilderment and nodded, can of peaches she repeated.

Yes if you see me and I don't know what is going on, you say, can of peaches. They have cameras all over the place and see what is going on.

She looked at him cameras what is that?

Did you see the little shinny things on the rocks when I move the sunlight around. Those were cameras so people can see what you are doing from far away. They see everything that we are doing.

Alcola looking around I don't see them.

No there are none here he said thinking that she did not understood what he was telling her. OK now about my walk about there is another compound a place like this figuring that she did not understand the word compound, where they take the kids.

CHAPTER 11

Camera Everywhere

Alcola face lit up you saw my son Krima, how is he, we go see him?

Yes he is fine, but we do not go yet, we need a plan so the people at the other end of the cameras do not know what we are doing.

When we go?

In a few suns right now we need to make them think that I'm under their control. I'll bet they will be watching me for a few suns. So I will play along for a while. But I'll be alright just playing but if I do go off you know what to do right.

Can of peaches she smiled.

OK now you know, let's go back to camp. Remember don't tell anyone about the cameras and do not look at them.

Playing the role of a member in compound one, till he figured that they would believe that he had conformed as a cave dweller, even went on a boar hunt with all the men.

Alcola keep asking about her son.

Two weeks later David figured he had played the role as a Neanthreal long enough and he was tired of playing unintelligent. Oh the sleeping with Alcola was good and the not working was alright but all the while he keep thinking of that scientist over there watching them. All the while he was planning on how he was going to escape from this place and make those bastard pay for what they are doing. The next day he told Alcola that he wanted to go over to the other camp and were still watching him they would just think he was going for a walk with his mate by now they should be thinking that they had paired up and going alone with their plan and might not suspect something. Also if caught she knew that how to reverse their hypnosis. Also he wanted to go over several times so if they saw him missing they would think he was at the other camp. He had work out a plan, just not sure how it would end up. But he knew if it would work it would take both camps and the other compound with the kids in it.

At the other Camp David slip in to the act of not remembering anything till he was sure they were out of sight of any cameras. He did see two out on the compound using his mirror. Griz just watch him as he moved the reflecting on the rocks. David had told him not to talk till later after getting Griz off to a spot David was sure there were no cameras. Those people who were taken the kids are watching everything that you do around here.

Griz looked around, I don't see them.

That because they have little things that they can see you from far away and you cannot see them,

That what I came to talk to you about, we need to work together and fight them and I also saw the kids!

CHAPTER 12

The Doors

D avid was thinking about how the men in white coats had just appeared out of the rocks. There must be some kind of a hidden cave, Also that they suddenly appeared at both camps. Also how they didn't have guns that would kill only tranquilize.

He put on his acting as if he was still under hypnoses and wondering around the camp with his mirror and check out the spot he thought the men had disappeared when he shot down their hovercraft. It didn't take long and he spotted a camera that didn't cover anything but the rock wall. He slowly moved over to the spot and looked around, not really looking like he was looking for a door. Now that he knew what to look for it was easy to see. It did not look like real rocks.

David sat there, just out of the view of the camera, trying to figure out how to open the door. When Alcola show up

What are you doing are you all right, can of peaches.

No I'm alright but glad you remember I'm just thinking how to open that door over there pointing at the rock wall.

There no door over there just the rock wall.

Oh there a door there, see that shinny thing up there that's one of those camera I have been tell you about. I need a way to make that camera to not work.

Why don't you just go up there and take it out.

I can't because if the see me doing that they will know, that I know that they are watching us.

Hay how about we get one of the kids to climb up there and take it out.

Might be the right ideal if not take it out maybe break with a rock.

Wait right here I know just the kid. She left and a few minutes later she came back. With one of the bigger kids this is Hime he can do it.

Tell him to climb up there take a rock and brake that shinny thing

Alcola told what she wanted.

Hime said he could hit it with a rock from over there pointing about ten feet away and not climb up there.

That would even be better if he could do it David thought.

I can do it, as he walked out and picked up a rock and throw it only missing by inches. He looked at David and Alcola then picked up another rock and let it fly, Bulls- eye. Hime smiled at the two of them and walked away.

As he did David gave him a thumb up and a pat on the head.

Now what Alcola asked?

We wait and see how long it takes to come out and fix it.

How long will that take Alcola asked?

I don't know but they will come, probably at night so no one can see them.

So how will we know?

Because I'm going to sleeping right over there pointing behind a rock David said.

I'll stay with you.

No you need to make it look like I'm staying in the cave with you.

David didn't have to wait long the second night , the door open and two men came out one caring the dart gun to keep watch while the second one fix the camera. After a half hour they both walked to the door and the one with the gun reached up above the door and turned a fake rock and the door open.

That is their way out David thought, but out to where? This was only one door was their more? Could there be another over at camp 2 and camp 3.

CHAPTER 13

Getting everyone Together

Now that David had his way to escape this insane asylum, but he had already decided that he was going to take everyone with him. If not he would expose them to the world. The next thing was to make a plan. He also knew that the first thing he needed was one of those dart guns. He hadn't seen any other guns.

The next part of the plan was to check and see if the other compounds had secret tunnels. So he needed to go and see Griz over in compound 2 but he needed to go without drawing attention to himself.

The next day he wander off into the woods with Alcola in the opposite direction of camp 2 then circle around the camp and headed toward camp 2. At the camp he sent Alcola in to bring Griz out, to a place staying out of sight of any possible cameras that might be all the while looking for a cave entrance. It wasn't hard to find it look just like the one in camp one and had the fake door opener at the top of it.

After of three hours of telling Griz what was going on about the abduction of their people? David was not sure Griz Understood all David was telling him after Alcola translated it to him. He did say that they would go along with them David show him the door in the rock and the cameras.

A Road You Don't Want to Travel

David's next stop would be camp three and Alcola knew that was where her son was, so David was not sure he wanted to take her there but there was no stopping her.

CHAPTER 14

Camp Three Again

David loses the argument with Alcola and they headed of in the direction David thought, he had gone on, to find camp 3. After three days they finally came upon the fence but not in the same spot this section had cameras, David almost came in view of the cameras he step back fast grabbing Alcola arm and pulling her with him, back into the trees. Then pointed out the cameras to her explaining how they did not want to be seen in them, they stay in the woods following the fence looking for the spot where David had slid under the 600 volt hot wire. They came on a sign saying that but not the same one that David had found on his last trip to camp three. So they moved along the line advoiding the cameras.

Finally the next day they came across a section that had a sign with the cameras that did not cover the one place David went over and check where he had dug under the fence it looked partly dug out after David moved the brush. Yes this is the spot but they had to dig out more and David had to explain to Alcola how not to touch the fence as they slid under it.

Once on the other side David headed toward the compound being more alert of hidden cameras as he remember that there were more monitors watching camp three than any of the others and that some scientist had said that this bunch had a higher IQ than the rest. So they were more obsessed with this camp. Therefore they had more cameras.

At the edge of Camp David stop Alcola from going in telling her she would stick out and the scientist might pick her out. So they waited out sight till someone came by.

An hour later a young lady came by,

Alcola step out to meet her Lorla do you remember me.

Alcola when did you get here?

They did not bring me I walked. Who is in charge here we need to talk to them, but we cannot go into camp because the people who brought you here are watching all of you all of the time.

Looking around trying to see who Alcola was talking about, Washen would be the one to talk to. I don't see the OTHERS, that the name we call the thing that move us.

Step over here my friend will tell you something so that you will know what is going on around here.

Loria follow Alcola to the place where David was hidden. As soon as she saw him David where have you been, I have not seen you since you show us that thing that killed the DIEA from three links away.

They saw me and came and got me and took me to their control center. They have these things called cameras and the can see thing that happen from far away.

If this is so why can they not see us here?

In the control room they said that they had sent the smart one to camp three so David figured that Lorla was one of them and he could tell her about the cameras and she might understand.

So as David, Alcola, And Lorla, work their way around to the rock cleft David could see in the distance as soon as David got close to the cliff he spotted the door they all looked alike. He stopped always back out of the range of the camera had Lorla come up next to him pulling out his piece of a mirror then told Loria to watch for a shiny spot and started shinning it along the hill till it hit the shine camera lends he did hold it there long. Then turned to Lorla did you see that shiny spot on the cliff.

Yes she answer what is it?

That is one of many of those cameras I was telling you about, where the others can see everything you people do here in camp.

What do we do asked Lorla?

Well first I need to talk with Washen. But don't go running into camp and get him. Remember the OTHERS are watching everything you do. Don't come back till almost before the sun goes down. We will be waiting right over there David pointed behind some trees between the main camp and the door to a tunnel so when Lorla and Washen came back the camera would not see them. Ok go now and we will see you later.

What about my son Krima, Alcola asked?

Oh he's ok get along with everybody?

Can you

NO not now David interrupted Alcola there will be lot of time later right now might get us in trouble. Lorla don't tell him about his mother ok see you and Washen later.

David took Alcola arm and pulls her back in the woods. When they were always back and David thought they were out of range of any cameras he let her arm go.

Why can I not see my son?

That is why I did not want to bring you. If the OTHERS see you or your son gives anything away and you will most likely never see your son. Just follow along with the plan and I assure you, you will see your son OK.

As the sun set Lorla and Washen show up and met David and Alcola in the woods.

Washen spoke first hi David have not seen you in a while. What Lora has been telling me there a lot more going on around here than what we have been thinking. And we have been thinking a lot. Somethings just have not been the way it should be, but what Lorla has been telling us, with this so call camera thing and someone knowing about everything we do, it sound about right. All of this was translated to David by Alcola, David had not been that fast on their language yet and there were a lot of words he did not understand.

So what are we going to do about this Washen asked?

We I have been thinking. Camp two has the older more experience men we are going to start there. That way if something goes wrong People here at camp three will not be suspected. You are smart enough to come up with a better plan. If we do get control we will come and get you because the people here in camp three will probably adapt to what is going on at the other end of that tunnel. And speaking of that tunnel let me show what I've been talking about follow me and only stay low and follow my lead.

David led the way and stop just short of what he figured the camera range was. Ok see that group of rocks there is one just like it in camp two and camp one and see that rock right above it you turn that and a door will open up behind is a tunnel that can go to the other camps but those OTHERS as you call them, can see that door. They know that people here in camp are smart enough to figure it out so they are watching you more than the other camps.

So what do we do asked Washen?

Just be ready to move if the time comes Alcola will come and get you, bring only your spears, and bow and arrows leave everything else here and bring all the people.

When is this all going to happen Washen asked?

Soon I don't know exact time just be prepared and remember that they can see everything you do and I'm sure they can hear anything we say near their cameras. And remember they have hidden camera all around the compound.

The first thing was to find his gun that was the last thing he did, before they shot him with the dart gun was to hide it under a rock. It was a 22 and only had two shells left in it. If it was still there, it took a few minutes to find but there it was it felt good just knowing that he had it. And get back to camp two.

CHAPTER 15

The Take over

Now the problem, how to get their attention, without just hitting the camera with a rock this time then it came to him take a branch from a tree and wave it in front of it block the view.

On the third night David afford pay off the door open and two men came out one with pruning shears the other one carrying the dart gun, both caring radios.

David and several of the men from camp two jumps out from behind rock and in a short time had the two uninvited intruders capture David grab the dart gun pointed at one man is this tunnel connected to the other camps.

I cannot tell you that the one that had the dart gun said.

David pointing the gun at him, yes you can and will.

Ha that just a tranquilizer gun he said.

I know but if I shot you in the eye the dart will go straight to your brain, do you think you will wake up after that?

No the tunnel splits up about a hundred yards back goes to both compound one and three.

Ok now how do you open the door on the inside?

There a red and green lite beside the door, top one opens bottom one will close the door.

David step inside the tunnel and checked he was right top one green bottom one red ,he check when he open the door. Everyone looked on in amassment.

David turned to Griz Ok get all your people.

All of then he asked?

Yes David turned to Alcola tell him we are moving to a much better place. They won't need much it will all be there new, with all the food you can eat.

David turned to the security guard any camera in the tunnels.

No he answered.

David pointe the dart gun at the guard I know that there is so you lie to me one more time I will shoot your eye out. Now how many guards are there?

Just me then he hesitated three only one on duty at a time we work eight hour shift unless we are moving someone from one camp to another.

Griz show up with all the other members of his clan. David said ok follow me as he walked into the tunnel everyone stop at the entrance. David stopped turn around come on what the matter.

David you see the fire? David looks at Alcola what fire?

Alcola pointed at the light in the tunnel.

David had forgotten that none of them had seen lights before. He turns back to the people and said, my people use them to see at night. They will not hurt you come see as he walked into the tunnel.

They follow but still looking at the lights Kind of dodging them as they passed A little way down the tunnel the felt better that the lights would burn them.

David turned to Alcola and explains to her the switch beside door and pushes the red and the door started to closed. Griz started to say something. David pushed the green and the door opened. David saw the golf cart but figured if the light and the door scared them then he had better left that alone.

David was hoping that everyone in the control was asleep and no one was watching the monitors. When David reaches the junction that split up the tunnels they were mark 1 2 3 they had just came out of 2. David stopped so did everyone else he turn to Alcola take two men go one and get everyone there and then come back and send them down this tunnel then go from here to that tunnel three and get everyone from there explain to them the lights. My son she asked.

He down that tunnel pointing at tunnel three you can get him and everyone else. Remember the door lights top one green opens the door red closed the door. Before you go translate this Griz come over here leave two men here to watch these Two pointing at the guard and the technician bring them down when everyone get here. Now when we get to this control door drawing on the ground a circle we come in a door here and straight to this door and bring everyone we find into this room. There are a lot of lights picture in a box don't let them stop you go straight to this room here pointing to the sleeping quarter and bring everyone in to this room. Alcola did they get all of this. Before David turned to the two men who were told to watch the guard and the technician where they could see him pointing at them you two then to his eye see those pointing at the guard and technician then made a hand in front of his mouth then David slide his hand across his throat hand pointe to the guard and technician. David didn't think Griz men did not get it but the guard and technician did. David then turned to the guard and technician to sit down and stay there, they both did.

When they got to the door David open it and everyone ran in only to find one scientist making notes at the desk. When he looked David put his figure in a sign of to be quit they motion to sit down. pointed to one of the men behind him then David put two finger to eyes then pointed to the scientist .then went to the door to the sleeping room and as he open the door two men ran and grab the sleeping resident and took them to the control room and had them sit back to the wall.

They had gone thru so fast Griz and his people didn't have time to look around. But now with four and scientist and other two guards sitting on the floor in the control room. It went better than David had expected. They were looking at the monitors. They could see Alcola getting the people out of their bed and moving toward the door and into the tunnel, then a few minutes later seeing her on another screen her wake up everyone and telling them to go to the tunnel.

David thought to himself they can see what was happening, and they could also hear what is going on. Once he could see everyone heading toward the tunnel he turned to the scientist still sitting at the desk he went over and pulled out the thumb driver and pointed it at him where are more of these?

I don't know he answered.

Well get and find some then you will.

He opens a drawer and pulls out five thumb drives.

There see, now you know as David went over to one computer inserted one then found the computer back up and up loaded all the information. Then to the next one it asked for a pass word David turned to the scientist what is the pass word.

I don't know David raised the dart gun there a lot you don't know that you really do know. You think if I shoot your eye out you could find out the pass word

568db/$

See you do know thing, you didn't think you knew .David punch the password and got a lot of information and video's about what was going on around there.

CHAPTER 16

News is Out

Now give me your phone is there a pass word for it.
    Handing it over no it is open.
    David opens it up and taps on the microphone.
I'm listening
Find me Wolf broadcasting in New York City New York.
HERE IS A LIST OF POSSIBLE NOUMBER FOR Wolf broadcasting, David went down the list till he found News happen now. David tap on that
A LADY CAME ON WELCOME TO Wolf Broadcasting is this news happen now.
Yes I would like to talk to Ted Donaldson.
Well he is in the studio right now and cannot come to the phone. What is your news?
Good he might like to talk about this a group of Neanderthal who have been imprisoning for twenty years by the U.S. Government have now taken over the control of the control center and we have four scientist and three guards we are holding in this us government secret experimental compound. Where they take baby's and raise them in caves and they have been doing it for twenty years there forty people men, women, and kids age range from one year old to twenty year old. The reason I said Neanderthal is these people have never been let out of the aria outside of three

Squair acers there whole life living in caves. Eating nothing but animals they killed with rocks and wooden spires and eating roots. Not knowing that this is the twenty first century. Having being born here they don't know what the world is like out there in the world all the while scientists study them from hidden cameras.

What do you think! you, think ted would want to hear about this or shell I call another broadcasting station.

What did you say your name was?

I didn't you would not understand

Can you hold on for a minute?

Yes providing the U.S Army does not come busting in the door.

David stood there waiting for what seem like an hour but in reality was only a few minutes he was about to hang up.

Hello this is Ted Donaldson to whom am I talking too.

This is David Richeson can you turn your phone on zoom? I'm about to show you something. This is the control room where the United State Government has been keeping forty people men, women, and children, for the last twenty years, living in caves. These people don't even know what it is like outside their compound.

One moment you say this is a government Installation.

No one could afford a place like this, three different camps with cameras all over to study how the people in the Neanderthal period live with no tools killing wild hogs with sticks spears and eating berries and roots. Then having scientist from all over the world to come and see these people.

What is this place call ted asked?

Aria fifty five 55 not aria 51 it is located somewhere outside Kingman Arizona and that all we know about it David answered.

OK you are on zoom.

All right turning on the camera and scanning the control room on the monitor here are picture of camp one the Neanderthal period it show the cave they live in and what the outside compound look like the next set show the other compound then the last is a set of picture of compound three more toward the Bronze period. Last is what the camera cover the wire electric fence.

These are some of the people they have keeping in the compounds.

Just then Alcola came and the rest of the people from camp one and two. Here are the rest of the people from camp one and two, now where is my son; OH there he is as she headed toward him and other mothers spotted their kids and went to them.

David came back on these are the mother who's kid were taken away from them and moved to the next camp.

Alcola is the only one who can speak English and only a little that I have taught her they have their own language.

I stumble into this place two years ago and have been held prisoner. They didn't know what to do about me stumbling into their little installation so the try hypnotized me into thinking I was one of the tribe and that I had been here all the time.

Don't know if you can show this on Television. David went to one of the scientist and turns the camera on him.

He turned away and hid his face. David said oh come now, what your name, don't you want to be famous, you will be on TV.

Next went to one of the guards, Want to give us your name.

No I guess not I would not want my name mix up with people who had keep people for twenty years. When these people had done nothing wrongs other being born then, used for a government experiment.

Alcola came up to David, what are we going to do now?

Well I think that the government is getting an Army together and will be coming and kick down the door.

Ted are you still there?

Yes he answered.

Can you get us a good Lawyer and some news people out here?

Sure where are you?

We don't know somewhere near Kingman Arizona. I'm sure if you follow the Army convoy. That is headed this way you will find us. We have no idea what is outside of these compound showing him the monitor's that show the caves. Any chance you can stay on the phone till they show up.

A Road You Don't Want to Travel

I have taken you off of speakers I don't know how long that will be. Here is my number call me when they do show up, do you have a pen?

I'm looking around for one. Can you believe all this paper work and no pen or around oh here one?

Ok 205- 215- 0908 call me as soon as something happens.

Nice to talk to you .before I stumble into this nightmare two years ago I watch you and know that this would not just be sweep under the rug or just covered up by some Government cover up.

Goodbye closes up the phone and turning to the scientist and guard, Gentleman shell we go in to the dining room and be more comfortable why we wait. How long it will take we don't know. We have nothing against you. When the Army show up, we will be release you. Unharmed provide you do as we ask.

CHAPTER 17

Ted Donaldson

Around three hour later from outside of the control center. You people inside this is a Government Installation you are trespassing on and need to come out now.

David got up well that was faster than I thought and dial the phone. When he hears

This is Ted Donaldson.

Hi Ted this is David Richeson Didn't take them long to get here did you find a lawyer for us and is there a reporter.

Yes and ten from F.B.I. here.

Ok I will leave the phone on just listen. Then He Picking up a white shirt waves it as he walked out the door follow by Alcola. Ok who is in charge David asked?

A solder step forward, I'm Lieutenant James Landcaster, of the United States Army and you are?

David Richardson David answered.

Well Mr. Richeson you and your group are trespassing on Government property and need to vacate this facility immediately.

Well you are differently not informing to this situation we have here.

If you will accompany me in side you will learn more. To show you are good faith we are sending out all our prisoners. Turning to Alcola tell then to send them out.

A Road You Don't Want to Travel

Alcola turned and saying something to Griz, that no one understood. The door open and out came the four scientist and three guards.

Now if you will come with me David said you will see why you are here and understand why we cannot leave right now. You can bring your sergeant with you and if you have any women with you it will help getting our woman decent to come out. Oh and about fifty hamburgers plain and twenty pizzas it will help.

The Lieutenant turned to his troops Privet Long come here, take two men into town and get fifty hamburgers and twenty pizzas then gave him a wink and a smile. He then turned to David and started to take off his side arm.

You can leave that on and the Sergeant can keep his rifle, a solder without his weapon looks naked.

Thank you buckling his belt back on, lead on we will see what you have.

I think you will be surprise David said turning and walking to the door. As he walked in the door, he step back and let the Lieutenant and Sergeant to come in.

See all the people wearing animal skins or nothing. Some of the woman having nothing covering their breast both Lieutenant and the Sergeant took a step backwards.

Nice costumes the lieutenant said.

David kind of laughed still don't believe that your tax's are going to this millions of dollars circus.

Now that you can recomposed yourself come over here to these monitor's please, see these caves this is where your government has been housing these people for twenty years without telling then what is outside that fence. None of them know what is out there. The united States government has been paying for this and brought the first ones here and would take kids at age of five to nine away from their parents and moving them to the next compound.

Well I'm sorry but my orders are to move you out of this aria.

Lieutenant Lancaster it came from the phone David was holding. This is General Bolton. David handed the Lieutenant the phone.

This is Lieutenant James Lancaster

Well this is General Bolton, your orders now are to do whatever David Richardson tells you to do, First thing is to get those people food, clothing, clean up and then and only then you get a bus and get those people to a motel or hotel.

Yes sir the lieutenant answered. And walk over to the door. Did those hamburgers and pizza make it here yet?

No came the answer.

Well when they do bring them in here. Privet Hanson and privet Bloor come in here.

Two woman steps forward, come in here the lieutenant ordered. As they came up I need you to figure out what size of clothes they wear. Then send to the camp and get them some fatigues to wear and you need to teach them about taken a shower

David picked up the phone, Ted are you still there.

Yes were all still hear and listening.

Were you able to get a lawyer and a reporter?

Yes the Lawyers name is Steve Sanders.

Good could you get Mr. Sanders to get these people some clothes they are not going in army fatigues like some fugitive. I'm sure that when Mr. Sanders get thru suing the government he will get more than the cost of some clothes back.

Lieutenant Lancaster gets Mr. Sander in here. Get these people into a motel and let the wolf reporter in and tell him he does not broadcast anything, without me seeing it first. Secure the whole place and nothing leaves that building but the people.

Lieutenant Lancaster was standing at attention this entire time "yes sir" and saluted the phone.

This looked kind of crazy but it meant

He understood.

He turned and went to the door and called out bring Mr. Sanders and that Wolf reporter in here. Are those hamburger and pizza here yet? Getting and bring Mr. Sander the bill.

As the two men came up to the door you Sander see the man over there. Are you the reporter, the man nodded you are not to broadcast anything without the General seeing it first ok. Sergeant, go to town and get a motel and a bus.

Yes sir the Sergeant saluted turned and left.

CHAPTER 18

What the government would do

Boy general we got our tits in a ringer yesterday.
Yes Mr. President they say this has been going on for twenty years now. I still don't know what it was all about but there are a lot of very important people and the big one is Doctor Lee. Hell I had to particle give that Damn reporter Ted Donaldson my first born to hold the story for a week. Hell they got forth-two people involved that not to mention that damn truck driver and or the damn scientists and two of them are not even from this country.

That was another thing how did these scientists know about this place, and I didn't even know about it the President asked? And how did they get the national parks involved with this giving those wild boars and antelope for twenty years

It was all new to me I didn't even know about it till that reporter Ted Donaldson call me and I called Dr. Lee who said we needed to get out there and shut it down and that it was more secrete than aria 51 and a group of radical people had taken it over and had a bunch of scientist held hostage. So I sent Lieutenant Lancaster out there with a whole platoon who drew more attrition to stop a bunch of people who have just sticks and homemade bow and arrows.

So general what are we going to do with these Neanderthal people who are forty thousand years behind time?

Well we were thinking of taking them out to the old Yucca army air force base. We still control part of it. Then try to bring these People up to the 21 century by bring in some teacher. As for that truck driver just pay him off and tell him to shut his mouth or go to jail for trespassing on a government insulation. We still don't know much about him or how he got the truck in there in the first place.

Well general this is one hell of a problem we are going to need to find a fall guy.

Well the best one would to be throwing DR. Lee under the bus to take all the blame. He had to know about it or even started this. He has been here for twenty five years and that's long enough.

CHAPTER 19

Welcome to the 21 century

The two Privates Bloor and Hanson show up an hour later with fifty plain hamburgers and the twenty pizzas. David passed out the hamburgers and show everyone how to eat the pizza at first everyone just look at them then Griz went over try one, then took the top bun off and another bite of the hamburger smiled then pointed at it and said something and everyone dug in taken the top bun off kind of like peeling a banana. Then went over to the pizza this was another story. When the cheese drip down his chin he pull it out and looked at it like it was a snake. Then it broke off sticking to his chin and chest. He jump back and pull it off then shook it trying to get it off his hand.

David went over and got another piece of pizza and pulled out the cheese and put it in his mouth. Good to eat.

Griz look at David and try the cheese and nodded his head and said something then everyone started eating the pizza too it didn't take long and all the food was gone. Then David pick up one of the bottles of water and open and pore a little out then took a drink and handed it to Alcola son and motion him to drink. Alcola started to interject but David stop her, motion her son to go no and drink.

He took sip and then drank half a bottle then looked at Alcola saying *twata* that was one of the words David new the word as water.

Alcola went over and pick up a bottle and try to drink it.

David laughs then took the bottle and took off the lid, and handed it to her the bottle.

She tips it up and spilled some on herself, turning the bottle back up looking at it.

David took the bottle and shows her how to Drink out of it, then told her to show everyone else how to do it.

After they did everyone was grabbing the water, Alcola went over to David you could have said something about the water be for you gave then all that food they were talking about going back to Como for water.

Just wait till they see the showers David said.

You mean the water that goes off and on it taste very bad. Ok for washing but smell very bad no want to drink.

Just before dark a bus show up Solder started bring in blankets. Then in came Privet Bloor and Privet Hanson with boxes of clothed private Bloor went over to the lawyer and handed him his credit card.

Might be some left over you can take those back.

No just let them take it with them.

It took two days to get the clothes on everyone. They were not ready to put on city clothes and it did not matter what David tries to tell then. But they did walk out to the bus dressed and clean not looking like the salvage's that took over the control center three days before.

Before David left he took the thumb drives that he had keep hidden he still did not trust the government everything seem too easy. He was thinking when they get to the hotel he would take Alcola and just walk off and get as far away as he could from this bunch.

It was quite a seen getting the people on the bus. The only thing they had ever seen like this was the helicopter type machine. And anyone that took that got taken to another camp.

David got on first and motion for Alcola to join him them tell everyone it was going to be alright and for everyone to join him and that it will be alright and that they were all going to a place where there was plenty to eat and they would learn what it would take to fit in with these good people and then they can go anywhere they wanted to, with no one watching you. But first you must learn their ways. This was not one of those machines that took the kids. Three boys and a girl went from camp 3 went to the bus. And turned around and told in their language. That it would be alright and that David always led us right. That is what David got out of it.

Everyone reluctantly got on the bus all the while looking around. David told everyone to sit down.

David sat with Alcola when they were on their way David asked Alcola what did Kanka say, that got everyone on the bus.

He said that you were a great leader and got us back to our family and you will get us all we want to eat and a cave like one with all those pictures in it.

We don't call them caves, we call them houses. They have lights like in the tunnel only you turn them on and off.

As they turn into the hotel the news reporter was everywhere, the Army push then back. While the people on the bus look on. Not sure what was going on.

The news was out until they started getting off the bus.

The news started getting around. They are not cave people they have regural clothing it was all a hoax, so most of the reporter started to leave.

David went in and open all the doors Griz was first went into a room and look at the door then closed it. The next thing Griz was bang on the door trying to get out David went over and open it. Griz came out and was not about to go back in. David went in and calls the front desk to send up the maintenance and to bring tools and take off all the doors and tools so that the army can help.

We cannot do that was the answer.

Ok looked around and spotted Lieutenant Lancaster. Ok I'll be right there then on the way out he stop and told Alcola tell them not to shut any of those doors and I'll be right back and we will take them off. Then he went over to Lieutenant Can you come with me we have a problem at the front desk.

Sure what going on the desk Clark answered.

They don't want to take the door off and these people do not want the doors on.

WHAT why?

They do not know how to open them and their afraid you will lock them in.

Well we won't do that.

I know but they don't, so we take the doors off or stay up all night and teach them how to open them from inside and use these cards to open it to get in.

I see what you mean I'll be right back. Ten minutes later he returned with three maintenance men who started taken of the doors and pitting them in the room. When there were three doors taken off and they were moving to another room.

David got Alcola to get Griz to go back into the room with a little persuasion he went in David followed telling Alcola to follow. We need to teach him how to use the toilet.

What is a toilet?

Come and I will show you and bring Girz. David took both in and undid his belt and pee in the toilet. While Alcola explain what everything did to Griz. David pulled down his pants and pretended to have a bowl movement. Then took the toilet paper and wipe his ass. All the while Alcola explain it to Griz. David was very embarrassing but it was about the same thing they did at Como only this time it was in a hotel. He did not want them just go in a coroner to relief then self. After that he told Alcola to have Griz to go and show someone else.

Griz didn't understand. David remembers that the ones with high IQ were sent to camp three. David told Alcola to get some of the kids from camp three when she had four boys and two of the girls David took the boys and show them with Alcola explaining they caught on fast so David showed then how to flush it. That might have been one of David's "mistake because all night long there was someone playing with the toilet flushing it" David told them to go and teach the other men.

Next he took the two girls into another room and had Alcola demonstrate how to use the toilet by putting the ring down David Told Alcola what to do and the girls watch then Alcola told then to go teach the other women how to use the toilet.

They were right the kids in camp three were real smart they learn the first time by just watching. David thinking he could probably teach them how to open and close the doors? No potty train was enough for one night.

Back in his room David was thinking, before he was thinking to get here to the hotel and walking away from everyone but now, he knew he could not do this. These people he had live with for two years, needed him and his knowledge to adjust to the twenty first century. He just could not leave them now. So in the morning he would start, Hell he already had, as he was fading off to sleep with Alcola next to him. He was again Dreaming of the fence and how he had crawl under with the musket face toward the ground then craw under laying on his back carrying the rifle and see the two small lights watching him,

Next thing Alcola was shaking him David, David are you sleeping.

No what going on he could see people from the light in the hall.

How do you turn off the sun Alcola asked?

You can't, oh wait a minute you mean the lights

Yes the lights Alcola replied pointing at the hall.

David got up and spotted one of the girls from camp three he waved her over to the lite switch next to the door and pushed it up the light in the room came on. Saying on it each time, then he pushed it down and the light went off saying off. Then he had her do it while others watch saying off and on each time then they wanted to try it. He motions her over to the bathroom and show her that switch and did the same show saying on and off. Then Alcola came over and did it off it is, off and on it is on, off and on, off and on.

David stops her and told her take the girl "winda" David learned later was one of the high IQS which was why she was easy to teach" go show the other how to do it. This was David next mistake. Everyone wanted to play with the lights half the night light all over the floor. We're going off and on and each time he would hear off and on.

David finally got to sleep when Alcola woke him up again pointing at the hall sun off.

I don't think we can do that, but I'll try. David picked up the phone and called the front desk.

This is the front how I can help you.

Oh is there any chance we can turn off the lights in the hall on this floor?

Is this some kind of a joke?

No they just learned to turn off lights and were wondering if they could turn off the hall light.

No there is a timer in the basement but it controls all the hall lights, so we cannot just shut off one floor. You really got your hands full up there. First they want all the doors taken off now to much light. Tell you what I'll see if I can talk maintenance can come up and can unscrew a few of the lights.

Oh thank you David said.

Oh don't thank me yet I can't guarantee they will do it.

Well I appreciate your trying, thank you.

Turning to Alcola they are going to try but the might not be able to do it.

Ten minutes later a maintenance man came in the hall with a ladder and started unscrewing every other light. Those that were still awake stood around and watch in amazement following him to each light he unscrew he didn't take them out just unscrew them far enough to turn them off and each time it went off they all said off.

David laughed and went back to bed and
Alcola follow.

CHAPTER 20

So this is what they eat now

In the morning the hotel brought in their continual breakfast. Everyone on the floor look at it wondering what this was? They had never seen this food be for.

David walk up and motion Loria and Krima "Alcola son to come up front, Then he picked up an apple show it to everyone and said Apple and took a bite, then he rub his stomach. Then gave it to Washen next pick up a banana show everyone and said banana, peels it back take a bite and hand it to Geiz saying banana. Next milk saying milk and open the box and show them how to drink it. He passes it on to one of the group. Now came the big one I will do this for everyone. . He took the little cup filled it with waffle batter and pore it in the waffle cooker turn the handed waited till they heard to small bell. Open the cook waffle, Waffle he said and put it on a plate added the butter, butter he announced. Then added the syrup and cut it in smell pieces offered the plate to everyone then starter doing it again. Adding a fork and handing the whole plate to Griz. And started make another. Passing it out with a fork and started another one and so on and so forth till everyone got a fork and a Weffel. At around ten o: clock everyone had a fork and a waffle and the apples and banana were gone. Taking the last waffle, to Alcola she except it saying: You make good cook and accepted it, did you get one?

No I will just have a bite of yours ok.

`That would be ok but no hamburger and pizza.

I'll put in your order for dinner.

What you just tell them and they bring food.

That just works with special groups like this one; most people have to buy food. We will get into money later.

Well the hamburger and pizza had to come later. For lunch they brought in a large pot of soup and an assortment of sandwiches everyone looked at David.

Ok David walked up pick up sandwiches and announces Sandwiches," they all repeated Sandwiches." and a bowl and held it out to be filled by the chief then pick up a spoon, spoon showing everyone, Spoon they all repeated. David went over and set down and started eating with the spoon.

After a few minutes when a few people had gotten their soup, David could see they were having trouble with the spoon. David stood up " Attrition everyone" they all looked at David He reach down and picked up his bowl of soup tip it up like a glass of water and drank it.

Foreveryone try it when they put the bowls down several said *nata* very good, Alcola translated.

David went over to the chief your food it very good and tasty, but you see this bunch has a problem using modern utensil .so more sandwich, hamburgers, Pizza, Burritos, and tacos or haw about a verity so they make their sandwich that way the can learn the different kinds of meat and cheese and tomatoes' thing like that.

Ok I understand from just watching thank you. I wonder why they didn't come back for more soup but clean the plate of the sandwiches.

After that it was finger food except for Breakfast it was Waffles. The second morning David taught them how to make their own.

The chief told David that tonight would be the last dinner and they would be going out to abandon Army air base but tonight we are going to have hot dogs and that it would be in the court yard and he would have his barbeque set up and barbeque forks and they can cook and make their own hot dogs.

That sound great thank you for all you have done.

CHAPTER 21

A new Town

At the abandon Army air base there was a guard shack at the entrance but instead of a solder they had a regular security guard inside the gated community there was twenty houses and a big rec center.

They were met by Mr. Sander the lawyer, he walked up to David well it took some doing but we got them set as best as we could. Each family will have their own house I noticed they only used twenty six rooms in the hotel so we set up twenty eight houses. They all have their own house complete with kitchen, bed rooms, living room, and yard. We have also set up the rec center with class rooms set up and three teachers. To teach whatever they will need to learn to survive on their own. And a large kitchen with a chief he will teach them how to cook till they learn on their own. A food truck will be here tomorrow to stock them up with the basic.

Holly cow you really went out of your way to make sure they got everything. Thank you

Are you going to stay here with them?

Only for a little while till I think they can handle it. I think that when they learn our language they will be better off.

Well both of the teachers are going to be here just to do that. The other one is basic math. Well after expenses they will be getting about five hundred thousand dollars each. There will be people calling and claim to be relatives.

Well wait here a minute, David went over where he had his things and got out the thumb drives. Then slip then over to the lawyer these might have somethings on them that might help you.

Where did you get these the government said nothing was to be removed anything. I have even asked for things.

Well it was too late to tell us that because I had possession and was outside before they said anything. I also planned that Ted Donldson of Wolf News was going to get a copy of then.

I'll see that he get them I'm a wolf News distributor. That's how he got me over there so fast. He made a deal with that General to keep a lid on it for two more days but there all kinds of rumors about the takeover of aria 55 a government secret insulation by terrorist you know how those people are anything for a story but no one has the real story.

Here comes your food now. As a Simi truck and trailer came thru the gate follow by a van with helpers to help unload. Mr. Sander stood up and went over to the truck and motions him over to the recreation center. An hour later a car drove up to the Recreation building and out step the chief from the hotel Refreal.

He went over to David. Glad to see you again.

Wow this is a surprise, how did they get you?

More money than I could make in two years beside these are old friends and they said to teach them to cook and that's the thing I wanted to do is teach. I think I had better go over and supervise that unloading.

Mr. Sander came over to David I need you to come over and sign some papers.

What are all of these David asked?

You have been appointed as represented all of them.

Well I didn't vote for that.

It is just temporary till they can speak for them self. Then you can drive off in your truck and forget any of them.

Oh good did they get my truck out there?

No but that is your replacement pointing at the truck and trailer being unloaded over at the Recreation center. They will have to use the refer part as a freezer for a while.

Are you kidding me?

No I have the titles right here I need you to sign also. You are also listed as one of the defendants you will be getting a cash settlement. Don't know how much they will be getting. That will be up to the courts. We have one hell of a case those. One more thing, there is a contract in here tapping the pile of papers in front of him. It says Wolf news has exclusive all fact to this story.

No problem with that I feel they will tell the real story of what was going on. You know all the other station will be making up thing they don't know anything about

CHAPTER 22

The Newsman Ted Donaldson

It had been three weeks Ted Donaldson had finely got to put out the real story about the takeover of Aria 55. He had been out to New World Village as they call it. Several times and met David who told him the whole story of the compound and how they had escaped. And they wanted to run a special. David wasn't to hip on that He didn't want everyone in the United State to know who he was. It was already bad enough everyone knew his name. News reporters have already been to David Son and Daughter house trying to find out about David .what kind of person he was "hell" they have said he was an Army Ranger, Cop, FBI, Homeless Bum, Cheater on my wife. Who had die five years early everything but a Truck driver?

One day the teacher came up to David and told him. Thought you said that a few had a very high IQ they all have above average IQ sure there are a few that are way high but all of them learn faster than anyone I have ever had as a student. They are already reading tenth grade level they all know English and speak better than you do.

The next time Ted Donaldson came out, David told him what the teacher had said and that he should talk with them on his interview. He had tried to talk to them before. With Alcola interpatient in their language this time Alcola was not needed.

Ted had his doubts it had only been three weeks since had been here last, and after the first question he just sat there amazed and even committed on it. Then went on with the questions about how they live asking about food, sleeping, life, in general. Loria, and Alcola son Keima, and Washen answer all of Ted question. In real detail even David did not remember some of the things that happen.

Later David learned from one of the teacher that half of the clan had what was call a photo memory. Which contribute to their fast learning? When not is class they were watching television or reading a book, one of the things the teacher taught then was what is call fast reading They could read a three hundred page book in a day and with the photo memory they could remember what they had read. David wishes he had taken that class when he learned what they could do. Already after three months they were reading at high school level.

David had been spending his time looking over his new truck. Mostly sitting in the driver seat dreaming of places he could go and places he had been.

CHAPTER 23

The court settlement

MR. Sanders stood up. Your Horner I'm not sure what is going on around here but all of our witness have been refused enter in the court house by Federal agents.

The judge turning the government attorney Mr. Avery can you explain this?

No your Honor I have no idea what you are talking about.

If I find out that you are involved in something like this. Your next court appearance will be your sentencing. Bailiff go with Mr. Sanders and escort these witness in here.

As Mr. Sanders and the Bailiff go out in the hall they run into Ted Donaldson

You made it in MR. Sanders asked?

Yes I came in the back door the goons out front would not let me in that way.

Well wait in the court room we will be right back with David and the others shortly.

As the Bailiff went by the front door he motions several more officers to follow him. MR. Sanders called David bring the bus around to the front of the court house. We will meet you there, and escort all of you into the court room.

As the bus came around the coroner the FBI agents were standing out front talking on the phone then the one on the phone

Captain David Belding

motioned to the others and the Homeland security officer walked to a car got in then drove off.

David was first called to the witness stand after being sworn in. Mr. Sander can you tell this jury how you found out about this compound called Como.

Well in the middle of a storm I found a lady laying in the road name Alcola I learn later.

Objection your Honor the government Attorney MR. Avery stood up he is not telling how he got inside this restrictive Government instation called aria 55. Then turned and said something only David could hear.

Instantly David looked around and cringes down behind the railing and hid behind the chair. Picking over the stand at all the people not knowing where he was.

The judge look at him, are you alright?

David not understanding said something in the language of the clan.

Alcola stood up and yelled CAN OF PEACHES.

David shook his head like someone coming out of a dream. Then Standing up and turning to the government Attorney. If you every say that again I will come down there and Kick your ass all the way out of this court room and break both arms and both lags do you understand you son of a bitch?

The judge bangs his gravel. Mr. Richerson another outburst like that I will have you removed from my court room.

Sorry you're Honor but you see when they hypnotize me so I would not tell anyone about Aria 55 and I would not remember anything except that I had been in aria 55 all my life. I heard them say if I every started remember anything else. They had a secret word to get me back under their control and not remember anything again. They must have told that Son Of A Bitch what it was. What they didn't know was while they were hypnotizing me. I added my own secret word to get me back to override their hypnotizing.

That must be the word the lady in the back of the room yelled something about peaches the judge said.

Yes they said since no one had missed me for the two years I was there. They would just use their Hypnotizing and leave me in there for every, I don't know about you but that sure sound like they were kidnapping me and never let me go.

I'm sure that after that long of time everyone thought I was dead, but on one could not find out what had happen to my truck and trailer.

The judge turned to Mr. Avery I don't know what the government is trying to do. but If you try to pull any more of these interruption to this case I will hold you in contempt of court and you will not see the light of day for your life time. Right now you will step down, till the board of ethics decides your faith. Turning to MR. Sanders from what I understand your witness came all the way down here from Kingman they will be put up in a hotel for the night and court will continue tomorrow at 10: o'clock . With a new government attorney!

MR. Averty stood up, that does not give the new Government Attorney time to prepare.

Well: you should have thought of that before you try all this other little games you have been playing .I suggest that you spend the rest of today and tonight get your replacement up to par at what is going on and I do not want to see you in my court room every again. Oh and I want to know who is behind all these interruption. Because I don't think you are smart enough to do all of this yourself.

The next day at 10 o: clock, the judge called the court to order the new government Attorney Sam Durham from DC. Stood up I would like to ask for a continence for an hour to discuss a settlement with MR. Sanders.

Granted one day and if I find out this is another game you are trying to play .I will settle this right then at 10 O: clock tomorrow do you understand.

Yes sir thank you.

This case is put on hold till 10 o'clock tomorrow morning. With no more delays is that understood Mr. Durham and you Mr. Sanders

They both agreed.

Then the conference room is yours.

MR. Sanders turn to David you will go with us. The rest go to the hotel.

`Ok but Alcola goes with me, for my protection David said.

As they sat down at the table MR. Durham started. We agree to all of your demands under the condition that NO ONE and I mean no one will degust this with anyone.

Sanders just laughed, so you want it as a big governments cover up NO way. The people need to know what their government is doing.

Oh now you sound like your employer Wolf broadcasting or more like what Ted Donaldson wants.

Not only that the people want to know about an aircraft that has a beam of light that can pick up people, like in a SYFY move and have they been using it before to fool people. I have been thinking about that since I saw the first one David added?

I cannot tell you that Durham said.

Well let's go in and tell the Judge we cannot come to agreement and we will bring this all up in the trial.

Hold off on that till I talk to my supervisors.

Sanders reach in his pocket and pull out his phone and slid it across to Durham.

I have my own and need to talk in privet.

OK we will be sitting here for one hour and after that, it no more negotiations.

Durham got up and left the room.

`Mr. Sanders turned to David what is this about an air craft that with a beam of light picks up people.

It is an air craft that they used to take kids from their parents to start a new compound. I had wondering about it from the first time I saw it till I shot one down once. So we know they have two of them. And I mean right out of a SYFY movie. It had me believing that aliens from outer space were doing this experiment.

Boy there is a lot more to this story than I thought Sanders said, and a lot more interesting.

Durham came back in alright you get what you want. But you don't mention taken kids from their mothers.

Two hundred and fifty thousand dollars each, taxes free they can tell their story, but leave out how they were kidnap from their parents and don't mention the scientist names.

Bull shit how they explain going from one camp to the other. You think that these kids can just walk away from their parents and can just forget then. And how about the parents losing their kids David asked?

Oh ya you're the truck driver you also get your truck and trailer replace.

Yes I'm the truck driver and the appointed guardian of all these people the Government Kidnapped so that you don't screw them over.

Does he have to be here Durhan asked?

Yes he does and he has the final say Sander shot back.

OK what do you want?

I want to get back to my normal life, and these people get a life you have cheated them out of. I'm thinking about doubling that. Raise it to Five hundred and Fifty Thousand Dollars each.

What are you out of your mind Durham spit out?

OH Ya well how would you like if someone took you as a baby and made you live in a cave, starving 90% percent of the time. Not knowing just over a hill were people with all the food you can eat but they were keeping it from you. And you had to stay there for twenty years. With people watching everything you do all the time?

Well we will just have to let the jury decided. And speaking of a jury have you looked at them. All those older woman you think they are going to side with a Government that has taken kids from their parents without their consent, putting then thru that for no reason other than to have people study then.

The topper of this is that their teachers are saying that half of them have a higher IQ than Einstein, and half of them have what they call a photo memory. That means they remember everything and they can repeat everything that went on in that hell hole. So let's go back in there and let the jury decided.

I'll have to make another phone call Durham said while getting up and going in to the other room.

"Oh man" have you ever thought of being a lawyer you had that Durham squirming in his chair. I'm sure he is going to come back with a new offer Mr. Sanders said giving him a thumb up sign.

A few minutes later Lawyer Durham came back in well my boss said they would agree to your terms but.

Sanders turned to David OH ya here it comes.

Hear me out Durham said. We agree to all of it only you don't mention any of the Scientist that worked there or where they come from.

Sanders looked at David and nodded his head.

David stood up and looked at Durham OK but the government pays for all of education including collage and our attorney fees.

Lawyer Sanders turn around so Durham could not see him. Trying to hold back the laugh and gave David another thumbs up sign.

Ok let's go back in and see the judge we can tell him we have come to a deal and Mr. Sanders do you want to write this up for the judge to sign David said standing up.

I'll write it up Mr. Durhan said for the Judge to sign.

No you work for the government. They have been known to miss place a few sentences Mr. Sanders will write it up with a copy for you and one for me before taken it to the Judge.

CHAPTER 24

Meet your Guardian Angel

David did not see the truck coming, until it was right next to him. All of a sudden it swerves right into them.
　　Well Hi bright blue eyes.
You can see. me?
No I have my eyes close but I can feel your present. I have known that you have been around me for a long time. Never really understand it till now. What happen?
　　You wreck another truck you're in the hospital.

How is Alcola?
Oh she is just fine a little bruised she out in the lobby.

So who are you and why have you been following me?
I'm what you call a guardian Angel. My job is to watch out for people and that has been a hand full. I think you have a death wish. Let see third truck wreck, one car wreck, and one plane wreck one train wreck. And I was almost surer you were going to touch that 6000 volt fence back at compound three, shot once, the way you play with that boat out in the ocean you should have drown a couple of times. Oh almost forgot that boat wreck at silver Lake.

You been around me that long? How come I haven't seen you before?

No but I know all about you and how you can see me and hear me. That been bothering me to usually people don't see us. Till they get a big shock .Like getting hit with a defibrillator, which they are about to do now. If your heart don't speed up

How about when I got that 440 volts shock up in Alaska?

That might do it. I had forgot about that one too, another one of your death wishes always playing with electricity

The nurse asked Doctor who is he talking to.

I don't know maybe you do you have sparkling blue eyes, but with a heartbeat of twenty per

Now you had better work on getting your heartbeat back to normal that doctor is about to give you a shot to get it going and they are hearing every thing you are saying,

David asked can they hear you.
No just you and they are thinking you are crazy.

Hay doctor you don't need that. I'll speed it up for you and David starting thinking about the Government experiment and the forty people having to live cave. Then trying to make him stay there too that raised his heart rate up to seventy five that always work at rising his blood pressure and heart rate.

Well needless to say that gave the doctor and nurses a real start they all jump back and stared at David.

Who open his eyes and said HI: I'm ready to go home now as he started to sit up.

The doctor put his hand on David chest, just lay here a minute. We don't know what just happen but you were just talking to GOD or someone seconds away from death. Now you are ready to jump up and walk out.

Well I don't like hospital people die here.

A Road You Don't Want to Travel

Not all the times just rest for a while, to make sure you don't have a relapse.

My Guardian Angel over there says I'm going to be alright pointing his thumb over to side of the room

You know they cannot hear or see me.

I know but it made them look and I thought it was funny.

Alocla stuck her head in the door doctor can I see him.

Sure nothing make since around here.

Hi how are you doing you known your truck was a totaled wreck.

I'm fine and I have heard it was, but it's good that you are OK. I'll tell you what; we will get us a motor home to travel around in.

CHAPTER 25

He is not guilty

David and Alocla got an old buss and fix it up as a motor home and one day they were camp by a lake David was sitting by himself fishing.
Well now that you know, you can see and hear us would you and your friend the lawyer likes to help us.

David asked who are us?
Some of the other guardian Angels.

What there are more of you?
Why did you think you are a special person with a guardian Angel? You are special in a way that you can see us and understand what dream your guardian Angel sending to you. They send them all the time people just don't understand that most dreams come from us and that we are trying to tell you something.

So what your problem that a simple man like me can help with.
We have a man who is on death row with an appointment with being put to death for something he think his son did: but in truth the son did not do.

What does he think his son did?
Stab and kill his sister and mother.

What does the son say?
Tell everyone who will listen he was a sleep and did not hear it or do it.

So do you know if he did it?
Yes we know he did not do it. It was the boy next door a Kenny Ashborn. He climbs in the window at night and was rapping the ten year old little girl and the mother came in with a knife. Kenny Ashborn the neighbor boy, took the knife away from the mother and stab her five times and Cindy the girl six times.

That's horrible and you saw this.
No Jenny the family Guardian Angel did but there is nothing she can do about it.

OK let go get Washen he will know the legal way to stop the excitation.

David found Alcola inside come on we need to see Washen I got job for him.

Are you alright? Last month you were near death talking to your GOD or whoever. I thought I was losing you now were running all over, is this that important.

Yes a man life is hanging in the balance. I'll fill you in on the way. Come on we will take the Jeep. On the way to Washen office David try to explain the situation.

Alcola listen with interests then ask how David knew all about this.

David started to tell her about his Guardian Angel but decided not to go in to it, by just saying I heard about from people talking and just got the feeling something was wrong.

At Washen office he listens to David story then asked how he knew all of this and that it was the nabors kid.

Just something I know or dream about and how it all happens.

Well first I need to go to the penitentiary in Florence and talk to this Mr. Burns want to come along.

Sure but are they going to let us in and talk to this guy.

As they walked by Mr. Sanders office Washen stuck his head in is it Ok David got a little problem Down in Florence and talk to this Mr. Burns It seems he needs a lawyer.

If David has a problem from what we know about problems there a lot more to it than meets the eye and he has that strange way of knowing thing that come out of the blue. Well if you're going to represent him he will have the best around. I pity the prosecutor go get them boy.

At the penitentiary Washen introduced him as Mr. Burns lawyer and David as his assistant. After a complete search they were led into a room, and then Mr. Burns was brought in with lag irons and hand cuff using all the percussions for a man coming off death row.

When the guards were gone Mr. Burns asked why a lawyer was talking to him.

David answered first; we know that you did not kill your wife and your daughter and that your son did not do it either. We need you to assign Washen as your lawyer so he can get all the files on the case and the autopsy. We are sure that they did not do a complete one. Once you said you did it to protect your son because you thought it was him that did it.

Burns asked and you know who did it?

We have a good ideal; all we have to it is proving it Washen answered. But we need the autopsy report.

What do you need from me, Burns asked?

All we need is for you to say that you hired us as your lawyer. And sign this contract.

Burns look at them I have no money. You are westering your time.

David answered this will cost you nothing that is just to make if official.

If you are right I have nothing to lose Burns surge his shoulder's where do I sign.

Washen pull out a plain contract, filled out the names and handed it to Burns pointing at the place to sign.

Washen pick up the paper and stood up OK Mr. Burns we will be in touch. Now we will go to work and you may not believe this but you will not have an appointment with your maker for a long time coming.

Back in the car where Alcola was waiting David asked Washam you always carried a contract with you and what with the comment about not to plan on meet his maker soon.

Washen smiled I have learn that when you come up with a problem that it will come out right. I have learned that all lawyers carry a blank contract. Just in case you come across a moment notice that you need one. I never believe that rule but they teach you that at law school.

That so they are prepared for in case they come across accident or anything to make a lawsuit and no other lawyers can steal their case.

Their lawyers why would they do that?

Why do you think that lawyers are called ambiance chaser David laughed? So they will be the first one at an accident or be the first one to sign someone to a lawsuit.

Oh I think you are making this up Washen said turning to Alcola.

I don't David's not known for telling stories but as they say sounds like boar shit to me.

OK what next Washen asked?

Well we need to get a copy of the daughter Autopsy.

Well according to what I understand the neighbor boy was forcing himself on her and if the coroner checks the boy could have left some DNA on her.

This is where a real lawyer goes to work give me a day I'll contact the original prosecutor and get all the information. Stop by tomorrow around noon.

When Alcola and David got out in the hall Alcola asked what this Dma and how is it going to work?

It's DNA and everyone DNA is different it in your skin your spit your sweat, and in your blood, all body functions. David was trying to keep it so as not to confuse her.

I get it if the boy was forcing sex with her he would leave a trace of DNA on her.

OK that is what I was trying to say.

Well why didn't you didn't just say that. Where do you get these entire crazy ideal from and how do you know what happen.

Well you see I see them in a dream and for some region it really happen the way I dream it and something tells me I need to check it out.

Back at the motel Alcola and David is watching television. When the Guardian Angel appeared *something told you that how it happen. Well how are going to explain me.*

I cannot go around talking to my self and coming up with all these answer.

She laugh you are doing it now.

Your girlfriend is looking at you.

What? David looks over at Alcola.

Who are you talking to Alcola asked?

I'm just talking to my self-trying to figure out how all these thing happen to me. It is like I have some Guardian Angel watching over me tell me what to do, then David turn to the Angel and flash her a smile.

What was that Alcola asked?

That was just in case that my Guardian Angel was standing there and heard me. You know everyone has a Guardian Angel watching over them. They watch over you and offer protection and are your guide when your time is to meet god. You just cannot see them and they talk to you in the night in ways of dreams.

Oooh you are my guardian angel I see you and talk to you and you got me out of the past and into the now time.

David looks at Alcola and said I'm not a Guardian Angel I'm just a lucky guy who meet you.

You may not be a real guardian Angel. But to those people in the compounds you are a guardian Angel even though it was a Guardian Angel that lead you to them, that the way we work.

The next day David and Alcola met up with Washen.

Washen said that he had got a copy of the Autopsy and that the coroner is going to meet us this afternoon. So they headed over to the morgue and Mr. Cooper who did the autopsy after he look it over said yes he had drawn a sample of all aria of the little girl's body but did not do a DNA test after the father admitted he did it. It would take a couple of day to get results and each test would cost a hundred of dollars and since the father admitted it no since going further. In the case of an execution we save all evidence. Follow me into the evidence room. Let see that report number was E4528LC so we look for that no. as they walk into a room with a wall full of test tube. Dr. Cooper looked around and pulled out three bottles. I believe this is the one you're looking for. We will have to send it to the state capital lab to have it check. It will take a few days to get results.

We don't have a few says can we just take down our self Washen asked?

Ya I guess it will be alright you being the lawyer and it does have my seal on it just sign for it.

Back in the car heading toward Phoenix, Washen asked his phone the direction to the state criminal lab.

The phone answered and gave direction.

David and Alcola watch in amassment.

Washen just laugh yes just modern technology. Don't know how people got along without it.

At the lab Washen went into his Lawyer mode and convince the lab director to do the test right away. They call it crossing the palm. In other words it is giving a hundred dollar bill to the right person and being inform that it will have the DNA results in one hour.

While they were waiting Washen, How are you going to get a sample of Kenny the boy next doors DNA.

David answered it won't be easy because we cannot just go up and ask for it without tipping him off that we suspect that we know it was him.

Are biggest problem will be to find this kid name Kenny that live next door, Washen asked? near as I can figure is it has been three years since we knew where he lived.

The parents still live there and Kenny is going to the state collage in Phoenix.

David Look around and there was two light mist with them in the car he figured it was both Guardian Angles. Kenny is at the state collage in Phoenix, David passed on to Alcola and Washen who both look at him and asked at the same time.

How do you know that?

Same way I know that he did it David answer.

I think at this point we need to hire a privet investigator and the frim I work for has a good one let's go back to the office and talk with MR. Sanders.

The next day they were sitting in the office with Steve Hooper the privet investigator.

David explained what they needed anything that has Kenny Ashborn DNA on anything and the sooner the better. And he is at the state collage in Phoenix.

OK I had better get going MR. Hooper said as he headed toward the door, I will keep you informed he said over his shoulder and went out.

Washen turned to David are you going to stick around.

Yes we will be at the motel you can contact us there as he held out his hand to Alcola in a motion to leave.

Back at the motel David turned to Alcola, well all we have to do is sit around and wait

You are such a romantic, I'm going to take a shower and then we will see what we can do in a motel room for who knows how many days, while we wait for that privet eye.

It's a privet Detective you have been watching too much TV.

WHAT EVER, I'm going to get a shower then we will not be watching television.

When Alcola came out after her shower David was lying on the bed. Alcola wrap in a towel drop the towel do you like what you see..

David had seen her necked before and had made love many times before. For some reason this time it did something different she was beautiful as he turned his head as to look around the room.

Looking for your Guardian Angel is she here.

No I'm not in any trouble.

As Alcola climb on the bed said, oh you might. Be.

A week later Washen called Hooper got Kennys DNA do you want to go with me to Phoenix.

Oh you bet I do were tired of setting around this motel we did go out to Como a few time and visited everyone a few times. I even got one of those fancy phones like you got still trying to learn how to use it.

I'll stop by and pick up in the morning around 8 O: clock.

Alright we will be ready.

The next morning on the ride to Phoenix David asked Washen what is our next?

If the DNA matches then we go to the state Attorney show our evident. He will pick up Kenny Ashborn.

When do we get to tell Mr. Burns.

They will have to go to a Judge and explain everything he well has to reverse the chargers. He will walk out of the court house a free man. I don't know if he will walk out with any apology or any money because he confesses. I know he thought it was to protect his son.

As they walk in the man who accepted the hundred last times held out his hand I was expected to see you sooner give it to me, I'll run it right now give me about an hour. You can wait over there pointing to some chairs.

An hour and a half he came out shaking his head carrying some papers. Sorry to tell you this but it is a perfect match, then he smiled and handed Washen the paper and a letter saying that it was verified by the state lab and you have an appointment with MR. Gray the State Attorney in a half hour down the street at his office.

How did you know Washen asked?

I don't know just had a feeling that I needed to rush and get you an appointment.

David looked at Alocla and smiled. She looked back and pointed don't even say anything about hundred dollars

Washen saw it and asked what was that?

Just a joke between me and David as Alocla said winking at David.

At the state Attorney office Washen laid out all the in information and told the whole story.

The state looked at everything and asked how did we know all about it and how did they know it was Kenny Ashborn before the DNA test.

Alcola spoke up David had a dream when his Guardian Angel told him who did it and where they could find the neighbor kid.

Let say this privet Detective Hooper found out about and told David, it will sound better the state Attorney said. Just a minuet I've got to make a call you can stay here and listen as he diel the phone.

State Prison Florence how can I help you?

This Howard Gray State Attorney I need to speak to warden Right away.

Howard what going on?

I need you to get prisoner Sam Burns He is on death row bring him to the Maricopa county jail, for court at ten o: clock tomorrow. OK thank you bye. One more call as he diel another number this is Howard Gray State Attorney, Sherriff I need your people to go to the State Collage and pick up Kenny Ashborn immediately charger is murder. He hung up the phone turn toward the three people looking at him. Mr. Burns will be a free man by ten thirty tomorrow morning.

Yes David heard in his head *I knew you could do it*.

David looked around and saw the two mist figure standing by the door, and then they vanished.

CHAPTER 26

Krima

Alcola turned to David since we are here in Phoenix can we stop by the university and see my son Krima.

Well I don't see why not, I'll just ask my new smart phone. Hello phone where is the university.

Here is the definition of a university, a unit of higher education that.

I know what one is I want to know where it is?

Then you need to ask direction, this came from the phone.

David sat back and drops the phone. This damn thing it probably watching us while listening this is back like in the compound with the entire scientist watching us as he tossed it out the window I don't need one of that. I'll just pull into that mini mart over there and find out.

David came back from asking direction to the university the guy wanted to know why we wanted to go to the university where the student created the earthquake. I told him it was, and he gave me this direction holding up a piece of paper.

Following the paper it was just a few miles away. And yes it looks like one side of a building had been hit by an earthquake.

David went up to a separate building that looks like the main office. And asked where he could find Krima Como and got a surprise answer.

Are you his father or another damn reporter?

Neither his mother out in the car.

Can I meet her?

Sure right this way as David started back out to the car.

At the car Alcola got out did you find Krima?

This is Alcola and this pointing his hand at the stranger.

The stranger step forward and extended his hand Jean Samson Dean of the University here it's a real pleasure to meet the mother of the most intelligent person I have ever meet you know that he found the secret to control light scientist have trying to figure it out for years.

David asked what do you mean control light?

Well it hard to explain everyone know light you see a light bulb puts out light it goes everywhere her son figure out how to harness the light you see the axially the power of it. You see that end of that building all rubble he did that with light.

Oh shit is he in jail we will pay for it, Alcola said.

No he not in jail, if fact he is in Huston Texas at NASA the space center. And we have insurance that will rebuild that. Your son will probably get a Nobel Prize. Like I said scientist have been trying to harness light forever all the ever accomplish is solar panels and then your son comes along and in less of two months does it I knew he was smart when he passed the AST test with only a grade school education.

You said he is in Huston Texas.

Yes at NASA.

Is he a prisoner Alocla asked?

Oh heaven no he went on his own will they hired him on the spot. Offer him his own lab, assistant, anything he wanted they would say yes.

Well thank you, Honey David said reach his hand to Alocla. It looks like a road trip

After a two day drive Alcola and David arrive in Huston Texas let's get a motel and go see your son in the morning.

After arriving at NASA they ask to see her son when Alcola mention his Krima Como three security guard show up and ask all kinds of question when they asked where he was born the answer in compound one. The question got more intense, till David step in OK enough of the bull shit what is going on.

MR. Como is the most guard thing in the place. There are several countries who would love to have the information that is in his head.

So you asshole are holding him as a prisoner here.

No and you are?

I'm known as David, Krima and along all the other people are my responsibility.

You're a Government agency why don't you check out with Homeland security or the FBI about compound one two and three. We are not allowed to talk about it.

The man who was asking the question said can you wait here for a minute while I make a call.

David lean toward him yes we will be sitting right over there pointing at some chairs. Takening Alcola hand and went over then sat down looking at him more like staring at him.

A few minutes Krima came in mom this is a surprise as he hug her, oh Hi David good to see you to.

Just then a man with a white coat came in motion to David to come over and went into an office. Turning to David let's leave them alone for a minute sorry about all the misunderstanding next time all you need to do is mention aria fifty five.

So Krima is a prisoner

No he can go anywhere he wants he just has the same security as the president. That boy has the answer to us going into space, not just space but anywhere in space with the harnessing light a space ship can go to the speed of light can go the distance from Earth to Mars in less than an hour that's 91,742 million miles. That just for starters can you imagine where we could go at that speed?

Back out with Alcola and Krima David wanted to check out if Krima was really aloud to go anywhere he wanted what you say if we all go out for something to eat

Sound good Alocla said and Krima agreed as he went over to the receptionist desk were going out to eat would you like to go with us.

Would like too but I still have another hour before I'm off.

David looked at Alcola and smiled, she didn't say anything just smiled.

It was the director in the white coat who spoke. There nothing going on Sherrie you go ahead and go home as he turned his head and gave David a knowing wink and smiled.

CHAPTER 27

Lema

As David, Alcola, Krima, and Sherrie walked out of NASA Krima turn to Sherrie why don't you call your roommate and have her meet us at Jen'o she might like to see Mon and David.

OK as she took out her phone excuse me for a minute as she step to one side and talk on the phone coming back, she said she would meet us there.

When they walk into Jen'o there sat Lema, Alcola recognize her immediately and went over and gave her a big hug so how are you doing over at the hospital. Are you a doctor yet?

No still working on my internship but you give me another year and I will be.

While this was going on David noticed the old familiar misty form behind her so he ask her do you have a Guardian Angel watching over you.

She looked at him what is that?

That is an invisible person that watches over you and keeps you from getting in trouble.

She looked at him but David wasn't looking at her he was watching the mist it almost became human form then disappeared. David just smiled just said that because you are doing everything great most people would take ten to fourteen years to become a Doctor you are doing it in six.

No I still have to do a couple year of residency they say I can do it here and that I'm learning faster than anyone they have ever seen. They think it is because I have a photo memory and high IQ. I think it is because I study more than anyone else.

CHAPTER 28

It was kidnapping

D*avid David wake up.*
　　What oh you, do you have a name just Guardian Angel doesn't really work for me.
It is strictly forbidden to reveal our name remember people don't see or hear us till the last minute. After they try to be revived them with a defibrillator.
OK why am I being woke up he look at the clock. What it is two o:clock in the morning?
We have a problem.
Me and you or you and your friends?
Me and my friends and you and your friends.
OK me and my friends.
My friends are the Guardian Angel of your friends.
WHAT?
Your friends have been kidnapped.
Again WHAT, when, where, how?
Washen yesterday and Lema, Krima,
Loria was taken last night.
Krima how that happen he can't go pee without someone watching him.
What was that about Krima, Alcola asked?

Just thinking is how a kid so smart could have such a beautiful mother.

Who do you think you are shitting I have known you for nine years and can till when you are lying although I like the flattery.

Where did you pick up all this language?

You are trying to change the subject what about Krima.

A well he is missing along with Washem, and Lema and now Loria.

We need to get to NASA.

How do you know, oh your Guardian Angel.

We need to go to NASA.

Yes, I know why are we not going now?

At NASA they went to the reception. Who do we see Krima has been kidnapped?

We know but how do you know it was a voice behind David and Alcola they both turned there stood MR. Cooper

Now how did you know Seem strange you come to visit and the next thing we know our super star disappeared.

David step forward. Knock off the crap. You said he was guarded and safe. Now you lost him. Well bigshot did you know that three other of our family were also kidnaped. All of them are just as smart and successful. So whoever they are that took them did their homework. It was all well-coordinated to grab four people all with in a six hour spanned.

What you are a detective now?

I would not have lost our friends.

HAY Alcola step between them, this is not helping find my son nor are other friends. David did your friend tell you where they are.

No.

What friend are you talking about, that knows about the kidnapping. Cooper asked?

David has uncanny way of knowing the future he calls this strange phenomena his friend

Alright they are taken these brain kids why if they can't get them out of the country they will kill them just so the United State will not have people smarter than anyone in their country now there only two country that would think like that one is Russia and the other is China. So our question is where are they, who ever got them were well organize because they got them all in the same day and they are that organized they must have a plan to get them out of the country. We need to move fast before they do. If we go to the police they will say they just out running around and wait two days before taken it serious. That is why we came to you MR. Cooper as head of NASA you can get the FBI involved right away call with a phone call.

Picking up the phone MR. Cooper turned to David we do know for sure they have been taken. Do we have an ideal where they might be?

David looked around till he found a haze with bright Blue eyes in fact there were several hazes floating by the wall, Do we?

In a voice only David could hear

There here in Dallas some kind of a ware house.

How did they get Washem There so fast?

They grab him yesterday around noon he was first one they got.

Is he talking to someone Mr. Cooper Asked?

Yes but don't ask, it real confusing Alcola answered,

David repeated what they had told him about them being in Dallas in an abandon warehouse.

Yes agent Swan this is James Cooper at NASA we have very strong information that one of our people and his three friends have been kidnaped and are being held in Dallas-fort worth aria.

Krima Como and turning what are the friend's name?

Washen Como, Lema Como, Loria Como Alocla answered.

As Cooper repeated the names then stop as he listens. Then turned to Alocla is that the Como from Kingman Arizona.

Yes we all have a house up there we call our town Como

Yes Mr. Cooper repeated in the phone. Then he pointed at David then Alocla pointing at her.

Yes they both said.

Handing the phone over to David, He wants to talk to you.

Hello I don't know if you remember me we met at the Control Center and I saw you at the trial. You were appointed Guardian of all of them. I'll pick you up in ten minutes

Ok we will meet you out front. Then handed the phone back to MR, Cooper Thank you we will be getting them back. Then motion to Alocla to follow him outside.

Twenty minutes later MR. Swan show up when he got out of the car he went over to David. Don't know if you remember me but I remember you. He reach out his hand full of pictures showing them to David are these the missing kids.

Well they are adults now and your picture is a little old except for Washen.

That because I got it at the trial. Oh we have Dallas and Fort Worth tie up, your friends won't be leaving there till we find them. I have a feeling you know how to do that.

What you think I kidnapped them?

Oh no David I just think you have some uncanny way of knowing things and you can help us find them.

I don't know all I know "looking around to see if there was some hanging around" is that someone got them and they are being held in Dallas-Fort Worth in a warehouse maybe something will come in a vision looking around again.

If you are waiting around for me to help you out, that all I know at this time, go to Dallas and we will find out more.

David are you alright Alocla asked?

Yes why?

You were just standing there for two minutes not do anything or saying anything.

I was just trying to think of something come on lets go to Dallas.

Come on with me Mr. Swan said. I'll get you back to that thing you call a home. Then you and Alocla can get back to your Gypsy life.

Have you been following us?

Watching all of you is mine assigned job, kind of your Guardian Angel.

You don't look like any Guardian Angels to me. In fact you don't come close to my sparkling blue eyed beautiful Guardian Angel.

Is that where you have been getting your uncandid information?

What are you talking about?

I have handled several cases that someone knew more about it than anyone and talking with them they say that their Guardian Angel told them so and that just before they died.

So you are telling me I'm going to die?

No, I think you have already gone pass that.

You know I think I'll use that, and then maybe people won't think I'm crazy.

Well whatever you use I hope it works because Dallas is a big place and a lot of empty warehouses.

We know a location that they are at on Camelback near an old church.

I'm getting a feeling that its somewhere on Camelback near an old church David repeated.

MR. Swan pick up his phone Sal look for an abandon warehouse near an old church on Camelback.

We got one around the 500 block the voice on the phone answer back.

Ok send me some back up I'll meet those four blocks east of the church,

Two hour later Mr. Swan, David and Alcola met up with six other FBI agents.

We have check out the warehouse there is active going on there a big roll up door on the front and two side doors in the back.

That's the right place back door on the left is unlock no one is watching but your friends are at the other door but the real bad news there is six men in there and they have ordered to if they can't get them out or something goes wrong. They cannot live because they are that big of a value to the United State.

All right here the thing if we rush in the kidnappers will kill all four of them. They know how important to the United State these four people are or at least they think that they are. Why I don't know but I do know they are in trouble and I need to go in alone

And that is not an option Swan said.

No it our only choose I know where they are at and how to get in David pats his pockets where is my knife.

Here mine, but I'm going with you. He then turn to one of the other agent you hear any shooting you come fast but not till you hear a shot. Ok how do we get in?

Around back the door on the left is unlocked.

How do you know that, never mind I don't want to know?

When they reach the door David pulled his 45 from under his shirt.

Swan step back where did you get that.

I've had it and I have a permit to carry it.

You carry a canon around.

You carry a 9mm David said. You shoot someone and they call an Ambulance, I shoot someone they call the coroner.

Do you carry that all the time Swan asked.

No only when I think I might need it, like this morning.

Do you know how to use it?

Not real accurate, but there seven shot to hit what I want. Ok we got to get in here they are tied up in front of that other door. I don't know if we can unlock it and slip out the back that's my plan.

You got a plan B Swan asked?

No just thinking positive plan A will work.

Ok let's go opening the door a crack and peeking in, it's clear come on as they slip inside the warehouse then staying close to the wall working their way along the wall to where all four were Washen, Krima, Lorla, and Lema were laying tie up David motion then to be quite as he slip over and cut the ropes. Then he moved over and try the door turned the lock and it unlock pushing on it didn't budge David stood up and put his shoulder on it and it open a little with a squeak.

One of the Kidnaper heard it and walked around the corner and saw them.

David look out

David saw the man raise his gun David didn't even think he raised his gun and fired. The bullet hit the man in the chest knocking him backwards he drop his gun and fell to the floor dead.

That when all hell broke loose. The other agents set off a blast on the rollup door making a hole as big enough for them to run in and the shooting began.

David stood up and hit the door with his shoulder and it opened. David waving everyone out when Washem, Lorla, krima, Lema were out David motion Mr. Swam who went out David follow at the door a bullet hit his lag and another in the shoulder knocking him out the door and onto the ground.

Mr. Swam pulled out his radio and call I need an ambulance in back of building one man down with gunshot wounds.

As they were loading David into the ambulance he looked up and saw Lema she goes with me she is my doctor and the only one who operates on me.

The two paramedic looked at each other and said OK get in.

As she steps in David you know that I'm not a doctor yet just an intern.

No you are my doctor. When we get to the hospital you are in charge. The doctor can oversee but you get this bullet out of me. I'm not going thru this and you not learn something.

At the hospital the paramedic rush David in on the gurney doctor and nurses meet the when asked what have we got Lema answered bullet in the lag and another in the shoulder entry from the back. Vital signs are pressure are 100 0ver 30 due to blood loss recommend----------- is there an operating room open.

She is my doctor nobody operates on me but her.

I'm an intern and he is stubborn old man.

Who are you calling an old man? She is doing her internship at whatever hospital and I will bet she knows more than most do.

We know everyone is talking about the child wonder even here, Lema Como and you are right.

Lema do you want to go and scrub up I'll supervise but he is your patient. One of first thing about being a doctor is to keep the patient happy and if this patient wants you no matter what you are the doctor. It will be a great time to learn.

I would like that if it is really alright with you.

It would be great working with the most uprising star doctor of today's medical world.

Lema got the one bullet out of the shoulder, with the doctor assent basic telling her what to do. The problem came when they turned him over. Lema had just started feeling for the bullet watching it on the x-ray monitor.

Doctor we are losing his heartbeat dropping.

Lama stop now something is wrong we need to study this for a minute.

The nurse said heartbeat still going down as they watch as it flat line.

Lema oh My God I killed him.

No you didn't paddle Start with two hundred clear.

David body took the shock the body shook. David said holy shit you starting a heart or jump starting a car.

Do you think that was funny?

Sorry lama that really hurt and I stop the pain but forgot about the heart.

You can stop your heart the doctor asked?

No it just does it on its own it always start back up a few seconds later. Did we get the bullets out?

The one out of your shoulder but not out of your lag Lama said.

Well I think the anesthesia ware off that why it hurt.

That's a first, the patient told me the anesthesia was wearing off the doctor said. Ok let's get him back under and finish up here Lama I told you it was not something you did because everything you were doing was right, you just got a very strange patient. But this is a good lesson in this. I have had patient who have this same

Captain David Belding

condition that the heart will just stop and start again it is rear but it happen usually they tell you about it. Let's put him back under add a little extra Lama you ok?

That was a heck of a time to learn that, yes I'm ready.

The rest of the operation went without any surprises

When David woke up he was in a room alone.

Well David you gave us quite a scare.

David went on thinking about who shot him. All the bad guys were shooting toward the oncoming men coming thru the roll up door.

David David can you hear me, can you see me I'm right here in front of you.

David was thinking that means he was shot by one of the FBI agents. Probably thought he was of the kidnapper. Need to see if lama keeps the bullets. He pushed the button for the nurse when she entered he ask if they had save the bullets.

I will check she answered as she walks out.

CHAPTER 29

Lorla

A few days later Mr. Swan met up with David I got a problem. That I don't understand I know Washem a Lawyer, Lema a doctor, and Krima the engineer, but Lorla, studying to be a computer scientist who is still in school. What does a computer scientist do anyways and why was she kidnapped?

Near as I know they design and analyze software and fix computers maybe make programs David answered, maybe because of her high IQ why don't you ask her.

I did and she does not know either.

Have you talked to the school?

Yes: but they are not saying anything other than she is a remarkable student.

Four months later after the kidnapping Alocla get word that Lorla was graduating with honors. A master degree in computer science and Mirasole has offered her a job.

A master degree in two years David asked?

I guess we had better go and see this graduating it will take us a day to get there.

The next day David got a call from Mr. Swan what have you heard from Lorla.

Just that she is graduating in two days and we are heading that way.

Well no one has seen her in three days.

Alocla got a call from her yesterday. Alocla didn't you talk to Lorla.

No it was her roommate.

She has no roommates Swan said and her not graduating till the end of the year. Turning to Alocla do you know who called you?

No but her number should be on my phone as she reach for it and handed it to David.

He opens it up and looked the last call read unlisted he said.

Let me send off to our lab they should be able to get a number.

Ok if it will help. You think she might be kidnapped again?

I don't know, but we have doubled the security on the others and at Como.

Let me guess you are our security David asked?

Heavens no you move around too much no one can find you. You did.

Only because I'm intrigued with what your dreams are, as you call them.

David just smiled he knew that he was more interested in his Guardian Angel then he was interested in Alocla and him. I'll meet you in an hour.

An hour later Mr. Swan pulled up next to their motor home. Swan looked at David what have you heard, in your dreams of course.

David looked around nothing.

So were at a dead end.

I think we need to talk to her school and find out what she was working on. There must be something that she was working on.

Why do you say that MR. Swan asked?

Well she is studying computer science. And she is a genies and computer run the world maybe she found something or created something, either way we need to go to the school, maybe they will know something.

OK want to take my car or that buss you two run around in Swan asked?

It's a motor home.

No it's a buss turned into a motor home.

Ok we take your car, we probably get there faster.

As they pull into the university parking lot.

David can you hear me.

Yes where have you been we have a problem here?

Yes I have been with Lorla Angel and she cannot find her.

What do you mean you cannot find her?

She was helping a person name Barbara who passed away and needed a guide to the father. When she got back to Lorla she was gone.

What when she got back

You don't think that since we are watching over you that is my only assignment to there are not enough guardian Angels to appoint one for every person. You are not the only person I have to keep an eye on. There are ten others I have been assign to, but granted you are the biggest pain in the backside of all of them.

Well that was an education and a bit of a disappointment.

Alocla sat looking at David then said, I take it you were talking to your spirited Angel and thing were not going right. Dose it knows where Lorla is at?

David sat there looking confused, NO in fact no one dose. So we are on our own let's try by talking to Lorla teachers first and she if she was working on something that someone might want, beside just her, like the Russian.

They found Miss Avery Lorla computer teacher. After introducing himself David asked if Lorla was working on anything that someone would like to have.

Don't know if they would like it but she had made three programs already one that stops spam and one was even a full game and the other I hate to admit it but it can hack into anyone's computer.

Oh shit that just added to the field of suspect of who would want to kidnap her.

You say someone kidnapper her, Miss Avery asked this is horrible. But how would they know she had made this program the only copy of this is in my desk as she walked over to her desk and open a lock drawer there was several disk there but as she looked thru them Loral's was missing.

MR. Swan look at David well I think this narrow are suspect list, looking at Miss Avery how many students know about this program.

Not many she usually spent all her time learning the computer or making a program didn't socialize much.

Wait a minute David said stopped everyone, if they have the program or disk or whatever this it is. Why would they want Lorla?

Maybe they think they need her password to open it.

Do they Mr. Swan asked.

I don't think so we did not expecting it to get out of this room. After they graduate all material belong to the university and are usually destroy. That way the student is not programs Miss Avery said.

Well mam I'm going to need a list of your entire student who has access to this room and their address Mr. Swan said.

But a course, I have the names. You will have to get the address from the administration office. It's MISS. Avery as she was going toward to her desk and waving at him with her finger to follow her.

David turned to Alocla where only Alocla could see him and lip sink and motion nodding his head its Miss Avery.

Alocla had caught on too and said so no, more like just mouth it STOP IT.

When she pulled out the list of students David reach out and took it away from Mr. Swam. Will go get the address and you can find out if Miss Avery knows anything about any students that might be doing something that stand out above the normal.

At the administration office David and Alocla meet Mrs. Frank who was not about to give out any address. David tries to explain that Lorla had been kidnapped and one of these kids might know something.

Ten minutes later Mr. Swan walks in got those address yet?

The lady will not give them to us.

Swan get out his cardinal with the FBI badge on it. Lady this is a matter of life and death. I would like to have that "tapping the list with his finger" address NOW.

OK you should have said that in the beginning as she went to her desk and pullout a big note book and began writing down name and address.

While they waited David leaned over to Mr. Swam did you get her phone number.

Who he asked? Looking at David and smiled.

Here you go the address of all the kids from Miss Avery class this year as Mrs. Frank handed over the list to David.

Looking it over David said where do we start?

Mr. Swan took the list, looking at it well there three names that stick out Lee, Okue, Sakq, they are all Chinese and china has been sending students over here stealing our technology for years. Taken out his phone and putting in the first address, that's just a few blocks away.

As they knock on the door David gave the answer there no one home .what is the next address.

And you know this how Swan asked?

David just smiled.

Never mind as he pulled out his phone for a new address, it's not that far away shell we go.

The same at this address, So Swan looked up the third address and no one there either.

Airport you need to go to the airport now.

David turned to Mr. Swan we need to go to the airport now.

Which one?

She didn't say.

Small airport not the big one.

It's a small airport not the international David repeated.

Swan pullout his phone again, saying small airport fifty miles around phoenix. It shows an airport called Phoenix Deer valley airport 12.5 miles from where they were. Swan touch the phone and it called the airport when they answered he said. This is agent

502 Swan of the FBI. Do not let any planes take off for a half hour. Swan hung up then called FBI

How can I help you. Swan agent 502 I shut down the deer valley airport need any law enforcement near there to assist will arrive in ten minutes.

Ok agent Swan I'll see who is available checking with local, sheriff and state patrol any more information.

Yes three Chinese girls one American possible hostage. Disconnecting from the call he turned to David I hope your information is correct.

Hope it is the right airport all I saw was small airport.

Swan look at him.

You know what I mean David answered with a look.

Arriving at the airport there were two stop on the tarmac with a sheriff car and a state patrol car holding the other.

In the building over there.

David looked out the window and saw a misty figure with bright blue eyes pointed toward a building mark with a big 2 on it.

Over there hanger 2 David repeated.

Swam drove by the sheriff and state patrol .there ok block off hanger 2. Both of them pulled in behind Swam and split up to cover the side and back door.

As they pulled up in front the main door started to open up.

Swan pullup in the middle of the driveway and got out of the car standing behind the car door waiting for the plane

David did the same thing from the passenger side of the car.

The plane door open and a man walk out and the states this is a Republic of China diplomatic plane. You have no right to stop us.

We are not trying to stop you we are just here to check your passports and your diplomatic paper since that you are on united State soil. So can you have all your passenger and piolet come out here with their paper please?

I will report you to our Ambassador and to your Secretary of State.

That's fine you do that right after you get everyone off that plane with paper in hand or you will be here a long time till I get enough people to tare that plane apart and the people inside fall out on the ground.

The man turned around and went back in the plane.

Mr. swam turned to David you sure

Lorla is in there if not were in a lot of trouble.

According to my information she is in there.

Good enough for me as Swam walk over to the door and bang on the side of the plane ok everybody come on out.

They came out the man then the pilot then the three girls all had their papers.

Any more in there Swan asked

No just us.

MR. Swan started over to the door of the plane.

You cannot go in there it is property of the Peoples Republic of china.

David walked over to Mr. Swan he right you're a federal agent you may need a warrant. But I'm not stay here I'll check it out as David step on the step and enter the plane. And looked around and didn't see Lorla.

David in the back locker. David went to a storage locker that was locked went to the door hay Swam get me the key to the locker or something to open that locker.

That has property of the people Republic of China you cannot touch anything in there, they are diplomatic papers.

Key or that pry bar over on the bench David said.

You heard him walking over to the bench and picking up a pry bar. Are you going to give me the key, as he handed David the pry bar.

He just stood there as David step back inside the plane.

Every one stood and heard the pounding and ripping of medal. The next thing they saw Lorla step to the door and down the step. Alocla ran over to her hugging her and taken her over to the car. Behind her came David caring a computer.

Now we will see how far your diplomatic immunity works for being a spy and a kidnapper.

Going over to the three deputy, two more had shown up and one more state patrol. Mr. Swan said take these three girls to jail till a U.S. marshal get here. I'm not sure you can hold that old loud mouth, but you can also hold that piolet. Charger is kidnapping.

Mr. Swan asked Lorla if they had the disk why take you.

The program cannot be open without a password and I set it up so it was my voice password protected spoken on my computer only. I wrote the program just to see if I can do it. Now I'm going to wipe it out nobody need this program it is all bad.

So why don't you put it to use where it will help people .I'm here to offer you a job with the FBI in our cyber dept. It is where we stop people from misusing their computer. You name what you want to work for us.

Lorla decided to take the job and on a salary less than those she over saw and stays there for twenty five years. Said the job was a challenge every day and she love it

CHAPTER 30

The Bus / motor home

*D*avid *do you want to help us?* Great what kind of trouble are the kids in now?
It's not one of your kids, not even one of your clan the mother is one of ours but Cara wasn't old enough to be assigned her own Guardian angel.

What you got to be how old to have a Guardian? Angel
Generally when they move out of the home then they get assigned. It's left to the mother to watch over their children till they leave home.
So what the problem that concerns you.
She wandered off and no one can find her.
So didn't the neighbors get to gather and look for her?
They did and have looking for a week with no luck.
How old is she?
<u>*Twenty three years old but she is artistic, she think like a ten year old.*</u>
So how am I going to help?
We have a lot of guardian Angels out looking for her and if we do find her we will need you to tell the other live people.
You saying she might be kidnap, oh shit I have had enough of that.
No not kidnapped just walk off.
And these entire neighbors and your gang can not find her for a week. How far can a person walk in a week, not far without

someone noticing? So someone must have given her a ride, that what you and your friends need to look for.

We never thought of that.

You mean for a week of looking no one thought of that?

No

Is there anyone missing from town or didn't go out looking for her?

I couldn't tell you there were a lot of people out looking.

Did she have any boyfriends or someone special not in the family. Did the police check her room to see if she was seeing anyone?

Not sure see that is why we need you.

OK where are you?

At Seaside Oregon.

We are at a state park just a few miles from you.

I know that's why I thought of you can you help use?

Yes we need to break down camp first. We can get there in two hours.

Two hours later David and Alocla pulled in to the police station parking lot. Going into the office David asked for the chief.

The officer at the front desk said, Can I ask what you need.

Yes we are from WATMC. Oh I see you have never heard of us. Were nationwide (Where Are The Missing Children.) We have come to help find Cara.

Wait over there I'll see if he wants to talk with you.

Few minutes later the sheriff came out and shook David hand glad to have the help but we have check every inch of the woods for five miles of her house.

That's what we have heard did she have any friends or a boyfriend. Maybe someone she thought they like her that would take advantage of her condition. I assume that you check her room for a letter or a picture.

Yes we ran all of that concepts still nothing. But you're sure welcome to look around. You will let us know if you find anything.

Oh yes and I hope it is soon and all turns out good, good day I will see you later with news. As David and Alocla walk out David lean over to Alocla they didn't check out her room. We will go there next.

David follows the direction he was getting in his head and a half mile away the stopped in front of Cara house. They went up to the door and introduce their self as members of WATMC and they were to help find Cara, and could they see her room. In her room there were several picture of someone David held up the picture as if he was looking at it showing it to the hope his Guardian Angel have you seen a person that looks like this. Here is her diary; here she wrote Richard talk with me today I think he like me.

Just then the Sherriff walks in find anything important.

As a matter of fact we did handing him the picture and saying found this in her diary someone named Richard. Does it mean anything to you not really talking to the Sherriff?

No I've ask and he does not have a Guardian Angel.

What do you mean he does not have a Guardian Angel?

Some of the bad people don't have a Guardian Angel they are going that way when they die they are that bad.

Who he talking to the sheriff asked Alocla?

To himself it's his way of thinking and puts everything together.

So if he's a bad boy he might have a record David stated.

I'll go check it out at the office good job as the Sheriff left the room.

Alocla looked at David you keep talking with your friends when other people are around they are going to really think you are crazy.

From Cara's house David and Alocla went the police station and check out if Richard had a record by matching his picture to a pile of criminal record. Not finding one David asked for a copy of Richard picture and a copy of Cora picture.

Back in their motor home David sat looking of Richard it seem like a small lake in the back grown and this being at the beach seem funny. So he took out a map of Oregon there was a small lake a six miles away. Seaside reservoir lake just stuck out in his mind and the closer he got the more he keep getting the feeling he was right. Jest before he got there he passed a small farm house.

Stop she in that house.

This is the voice David heard in his head. He stopped the bus at the road and started to walk up to the house.

He was meet half way to the door by a man with a gun; yes it was the same person that he had a picture setting on his dash: Richard.

Hi I didn't mean to bother you but my motor home broke down I need to call a tow truck can I use your phone.

Richard answered I don't have a phone so get off my property and that not a motor it a bus.

David walked back to the bus and got his 45 and started walking up the road till he got around the corner them when he was out of sight of the house he started over to the back of the house. Alright Blue Eyes I need you to tell me where Richard is at in the house and where is Cora.

Richard is in front room watching television Cora is laying on the floor by the bed she looks bad. The dog is tied up in the back yard.

Dog David stopped.

I can handle that one keep going.

David arrived at the back yard and saw the mist like figure kneeling petting the dog.

The dog just watches him as David open the gate and walked to the back door. Richard had a big dog out back so the door was unlocked. As David slipped in and looked around, Richard was watching with his back to David. David looks around for something to knock him out. The best he found was a heavy water pitcher. Going up behind Richard and hitting as hard as he can with it.

Richard went forward but came up the gun. Well that didn't go like it does on television, David pulled out his gun pointing at Richard. Put it down if you point at me you will be dead before you can pull the trigger. Let's go out the front door once out there David ordered him down on the ground hands behind your back

Alocla started coming over NO, David stopped her bring the duct tape from the tool box.

Richard kicked knocking him off balance. Then jump up and hit David before he could catch himself.

Richard move in for another hit David was ready this time and hit him with a right in the middle of the chest.

As Richard was catching his breath, David hit him right on the chin and he drop to the ground out cold. Like on television hard head but a glass jaw. David said to himself.

As Alocla came up with the duct tape David told her check on Cora in the bedroom. I'll take care of this slim ball.

A few minutes later as David was headed toward the house he meets Alocla and Cora coming out the door Cora looked really beat up.

They help Cora to the bus Alocla asked where is Richard?

On the jeep that they towed behind the back of the bus I didn't want that thing riding with us.

When they were half way in to Seaside David called 911.

911 what is your emergency.

I need the sheriff office we are bringing in Cora and Richard.

One moment please.

Hello this is Sherriff Turner.

Hello Sherriff we are bring in Cora and she is beat up bad were taking her to the hospital. We also have her boyfriend can you meet us at the hospital.

Where are you at?

We are about five miles south of town on HI way 101.

I'll Meet you at the city limit you still in that bus.

It's a motor home with a jeep towing behind.

At the city limit David was met by the sheriff and one other car and they escorted David to the hospital. And the doctors and nurse help Cora in to the hospital.

Meanwhile the sheriff stood by the jeep with the man duct tape to the hood with his pants pulled down mooning everyone.

Was this your ideal of a joke?

No just wanted those men in prison to know what we will be sending them.

The Sheriff laughed ok. Turning to the deputy cut him loose and put him in your car and take him down and book him. We will talk to the district Attorney on all of the charges.

Turning to David and a really big thank you to you and the WATMC or WAMC you called it today.

David just smiled and wave Alocla to get in the motor home/BUS and they drove off.

CHAPTER 31

The fire

David and Alocla were in their motor home in a campground in Washington getting ready to go south with the other Snowbirds as winter was coming on. When the phone rang Alocla looked at David you want to answer that we don't get any calls unless there is trouble somewhere.

Not all the time as David picks up the phone. Hello this is David.

David glad I got a hold of you this is your lawyer Sanders; we have some strange things going on up here in Como. Washen said not to bother you but we have had several unexplained fires around here.

What do you think I can do?

Don't know but we have been hearing about your adventure and helping people out all over the country. I thought you might know how to do something.

OK we will be stopping by in a few days.

David and Alocla rolled into Como two days later and were met by friends. They set up their motor home in the RV Park. Then David walk over to the burned out grocery store If someone did this on purpose, they did a good job of making sure, that there was nothing left to save including the building. Next he went over to the gift shop it was the same the fire destroy everything. As he turns to go he met Washen.

What did the fire department say started it?

David good to see you again, I know looks bad.

They did say it might be faulty wiring.

It' a new building the building inspector should have seen it. I think I will go down and talk with him.

We, will go down and talk with him this sounds like a law suit to me if someone put in faulty wire. The same contractor built most of the building and if they used faulty wiring it might be in all of the buildings.

OK I may need a lawyer. Let's go talk to the fire inspector. You know maybe we need our own fire dept. instead of depending on the county. Their all volunteers even some of our people are on it.

At Kingman David and Washen walk into the central fire station we would like to talk with your fire investigator on the fire at Como.

That would be Steve Hofman I believe he is up in his office. I'll check as he pick up the phone and talks a minute later yes he up there just go up the stairs there pointing at the stairs first door on the left.

David thanks him and headed toward the stairs with Washen right behind him.

At the top of the stair they were meet by Steve Hofman, who introduce himself, and you are?

I'm David Richeson the court ordered guardian of the Como family and this is Attorney Washen Como.

Oh yes I have heard of both of you come on into my office.

David started, about these fires.

Yes faulty wiring.

David just sat there looking at him, for ten seconds. Before speaking Lets not start off with a bunch of bull shit. We both know that there is foul play going on here. If as you say faulty wiring. Then you should be investigating the contractor or the building inspector. I have been two both sights and I hope you don't think I'm dumb. A electric fire dose not destroy everything in a building and you can still see the tacks where the balloons filled with gasoline were hanging.

Hofman lean back in his chair, yes I see that our faulty wiring story will not work basically that story was to keep people from panicking. We are investigating Arson we have been working on who would profit from the fires out at Come we have the police checking into it officer Bennent is handling it I'll call him and tell him to keep you in the loop and you can talk to him.

David stood up reach out to shake Hofman hand. Thank you for being honest with us.

Hoffman taken David hand shake I'm sorry that I thought we were dealing with some cave people.

David held back of hauling off and knocking Hoffman on his ass.

Washen was not as nice he except the hand shake and squeeze it as hard as he could. Those cave people as you call them out there are a hell of a lot smarter than ninety five percent of the people in this town and that include you. Then he turned and walked out.

David saw and heard Washen actions, outside David gave him a double thumb up. David was glad it was their lawyer that did it. He was sure if he did it they would be sitting in jail right now. Well let's go and talk this officer Bennent, and see what they have.

At the police station David and Washen located officer Bennent and introduce them self. Yes we would like to know what progress is being made on the fire out at Como.

That's still under investigation I can't give out that information.

He is the court ordered guardian to these people at Como and is responsible for all of their welfare. If we have to go to court and get a court order I'm sure the judge would not be happy and want to know what is being hidden from the Guardian.

Now I know who you are your that boy wonder Attorney who saved Burns.

Washen just smiled and I know the law and the rights of a Guardian so now what information do you have.

Come over to my desk. As he pulled out a folder and open it. This is the torch man Dan Lang set both fires fit his signature, but we can't prove it. We also do not know who paid him or why burn these two building. Now you know what we know.

OK thank you keep us inform please, David turned to leave.

Washen handed him his card if you cannot get a hold of David call me thank you.

Outside David told Washen will we didn't get much information except who to look out for and they are investigating the fires.

We also learned the fire inspector is an idiot Washen added.

Speaking lets go back and talk the fire chief about a fire dept. out at Como.

For the next three weeks David and Alocla stayed around Como while a construction crew came out and tore down building and started rebuilding's the stores.

One night David was just getting ready for bed When

David there a man out at the new construction site and I think he has bad intentions.

David grabs his gun and ran out still in his underwear and met the man coming out the door. He had seen this man before it was the man in the picture in the file on officer Bennent desk Dan Lang.

David he has a gun.

David spotted the gun as he was bringing it up. But David fired first hitting the man in the shoulder of his gun hand the force of the 45 shot knock the gun away from him and knock the man down.

David kick Dan Lang gun away. Alright who hired you to burn down our store?

Screw you call me a doctor.

I don't know that's a pretty big hole and you're losing a lot of blood. Now who hired you to burn down our store?

By now people were coming around.

David put his foot on the Dan shoulder and presses down.

Dan screams out.

Alocla came up David what are you doing?

Just then the new building burst into flame.

David grab Lang lag and drug him off the porch and into the road away from the fire.

Lang screaming all the way I'm going to sue you.

No you are going to die from lack of blood unless you tell me who hired you.

I need a doctor.

No you are going to need a corner unless you tell me who hired you.

David what are you doing Alocla your hurting him.

This is the scum bag that burned our store and I'm going to find out who hired him to do it.

Alocla walk over to Lang lying on the ground OK scum bad as she kicks him. Who hired you to burn down our store?

Lang was about to say something.

Alocla kick him again you were thinking of lying to me now who hired you.

Keep that BITCH away from me.

Alocla kick him again, I don't like that langrage.

Are you feeling weak that from lack of blood David asked better tell us who hired you before you pass out?

Ok ok call the doctor.

Who hired you?

Jason Simmons now calls me an ambulance.

Why did he hire you?

He wants this land now call me an ambulance

Just then vehicles flashing lights and siren turn into the main entrance.

OH that bad it's the fire dept. came to put out the fire you started. Now you want me to call you an ambulance tell me why this Jason Simmons wants our land. I don't know he never said.

Just then two paramedic show up and started working on Dan Lang

You BASTER you had already call them.

Yes we did and also called officer Bennent

David spotted the fire chief yes I think we do need a local fire dept.

One of the paramedic came by it was just a scratch he going to be alright.

Ya it didn't look that bad, thank you.

Hay officer Bennet who is Jason Simmons?

He is some big shot in the oil business.

He is the one who hired our buddy Dan Lang to get our land.

Maybe you better have it check out.

That night as David and Alocla were standing outside looking at the burnt building Alocla asked what is a BITCH.

It's a female dog.

And he calls you a BASTARD.

It's a male dog

CHAPTER 32

Missing a Guardian Angel

David got a few minute.
    For you blue eyes I have as many minute's as you want, what going on

See that young man over there. We have lost Alice his Guardian Angles.

What you have lost a guardian Angle, how does that happen?

Doesn't happen that often, but it does happen.

What do you expect me to do?

Talk to him and find out where he has been.

David walked over to him, HI you look lost can I help you.

Yes I'm not sure where I am

You're in Yuma Arizona where were you before?

I was at Mittry Lake there was a big flash and the next thing, I was here.

Were there some other people with you?

No I was alone just looking at the Lake.

How did you get to the lake?

I drove my car.

Is your car still there?

I guess so

Well would like a ride back out there and get it.

Boy that would be great if you don't mind.

Come on I heard it was good fishing out there.

As they walked toward the motor home he asked is that your bus.

It's a motor home we have converted it.

They met Alocla come out honey this is I don't think I caught your name looking at the stranger.

Dave Beld the stranger answered.

Well this is my wife Alocla this is Dave and needs a ride out to Mitty Lake and pick up his car.

How he get into town without his car.

He don't know probable from drinking. But I told we would give him a ride back out.

OK we have never been there before.

I have heard there good fishing we may stay a day or too.

They drove out to the lake and there was Dave car and the lake but there was no water in the lake a few fish lying in some wet sand. Other than that there was nothing that made it look like a lake.

What happen to the water Dave said not to anyone in particular as he looks at the dry lake?

While looking at the lake a truck full of soldiers show up the leader went to David ,Dave, and Alocla.

What are you all doing here?

David step up we met this man in Yuma and need a ride out here to this lake to get his car and do some fishing.

Well as you can see there is no fishing. Now turning to Dave what were you doing here?

I was tired of driving and saw this lake on my GPS and pulled over to sleep then there was a flash of light and the next thing I knew I was in Yuma without my car.

OK you and her can go pointing to David and Alocla. You are going with us pointing at Dave.

Why what did I do Dave asked.

This is a restricted area, you were trespassing.

David just had to step in, restricted area I didn't see any signs.

The soldier looked at David you better get in your bus and get out of here while you can.

It's a motor home not a bus. David said then saw the look the soldier gave, ok were getting in our bus and leaving. Dave we will see you later.

Well I hope so, thanks for the ride.

David drove out to the HI way then pulled over. Hay Blue eyes are you still out there.

Yes David

Do you know what is going on?

No just then a tow truck turned off the HI way onto the road to the lake.

Half hour later came out with Dave car with the army truck right behind it with Dave sitting in the middle.

Hay blue eyes was your friend his GA with him.

NO she is still missing and I'm glad you didn't mention her name that where I broke one of the main rules; never give out a name of a Guardian Angel.

I think we need to find our friend a lawyer. As David pick up his phone and calls Washen. Hi guy you busy, we have a problem the army just pick up one of our friends and probably took him to the base out here at the Yuma base his name is Dave Beld could you check it out for us.

I'll get right on it you say the name is Dave Beld I'll get back to you later.

Washen called two days later. Your friend was hard to find but I did he is at the US Army Yama Proving Grounds they would not tell us much on why they are holding him accept that he was trespassing. I'll go down tomorrow if it is only trespassing I'll get him out if something else I'll find out. It all sounded funny to me. What do you think is going on?

We have no ideal; but we know that there were no signs saying no trespassing. There some around, only none on the road going to the lake where there is no water, when the day before there was.

Captain David Belding

We are camp north of there on the BLM land. Let us know if you need us.

The next day Washen show up at the gate to the Proving Grounds and informed them he was here to see his client Dave Beld and was stopped the guard called in and told him to wait someone would be right out. Soon a jeep pulled up and asked Washen what he wanted with Dave Beld.

I have heard that you were holding him for trespassing but I have also checked with the court and you have never charge him with anything. So if you do not charge him now, he will be leaving with me. And his car will be return to him also.

We are holding for act of terrorism he blows up a lake.

Washen almost laughed are you serious blow up a lake. Not a building but a lake. Do you mind telling how he blows up a lake?

Yes I do mind.

OK I will be right back with a court order of Relics. Can you imagine the look on the judge face?

That you are holding a man on terrorism for blowing up a lake? Good day I'll be see you soon.

Washen went to a superior court Judge in phoenix with a court order to relics Dave Beld or file a charge of something other terrorism or trespassing and blowing up a lake. If not to give him all the evidence they have against Dave Beld.

The next day the judge reading over Washen petition smiled is this for real he asked? Bailiff

Contact the base and have them contact me before 4 o'clock today or I will sign this petition.

At 4 o'clock that Day David, Alocla, and Washen were at the court house.

The judge seeing them made the next case theirs. I'm going to sign your petition but the Army said that you won't need it that MR. Beld will meet you at the main gate.

David, Alocla and Washen went to the main gate at the US Army Proving Grounds and told them they were here to pick up Dave Beld.

A Road You Don't Want to Travel

They were told to wait over on the side of the road. Ten minutes later a jeep pulled up and Dave climb out and look around till Washen waved him over as he got in David asked where is your car?

I don't know he answered.

Washen got out of their car and walked over to the guard shack and asked where is Mr. Belds car.

The guard picks up the phone and asked.

Then turned to Washen nobody knows. Washen handed the guard his business card tell whoever you talk to on the other end of that phone that if they don't have MR. Beld car down here at the gat by noon tomorrow. I will be back in court at 1 o'clock. Washen turned and walk to the car.

Hi Mr. Beld I'm Washen Como your attorney welcome out, We will stay in town tonight and get your car tomorrow.

Who are you people?

Just someone that like to help people out and when Alocla and I saw the Army haul you off we called one our friends who happen to be the best lawyer in the state to help you out. So what was that all about like all the water in a lake disappearing.

When they pick me up it was strange first they said they had to sanitize me. Then ask me all kinds of question like who was the first President, where I born, was I an American citizen. They told me if I ever talk about what I saw that I would again be arrested and never see the light day.

I told I them didn't see anything except their jail.

Well they lie to you this is a country of free speech protected by the first amendment of the constitution of the United State.

Well I don't know what to tell, there was a flash of bright light and the next thing I'm in Yuma with no car, where you met me.

I wonder if it some government experiment because once there was water in the lake next day there no water in the lake. Now I don't know but it sure looks strange to me David said.

The government does not do experiments like that.

David, Alocla, and Washen all look at each other and all said at the same time YES THEY DO.

THE LAKE IS WHERE ALICE DISPAIRED the LAST PLACE SHE WAS HEARD FROM.

The water is not the only thing missing from the lake you say you don't know how you got to Yuma and didn't know where you were at maybe someone is in a place where they don't know where they are at.

We got the word out everyone is looking all-around for 500 miles she just no here.

I wonder where the water went.

The army is wondering that too. They are saying there was a UFO sighting at the lake. That is why they show up and think Dave Beld had something to do with it. But he does not.

Well that's good to know and explains why they held him.

Who are you talking to Dave asked?

He talks to himself all the time that how he comes up with answers Alocla said looking at Washen.

David realized he had said that out loud. Well the only thing I can think of is this might be some UFO that they don't want anyone to say anything about. And when they suck up the water, I wonder could they suck something else up like fish and other things?

Never heard of it happening before but of course never heard of OFU stealing water either.

It might be true because there only a few fish left in the lake.

They went into Yuma and check into a motel to wait till morning and get Dave's car. They were watching Ted Donaldson on Bear news. Bear news special report a lake in southern Arizona disappear and repaired two days later three hundred miles north in Utah.

Scientist is saying that a subterranean channel open up and the water went thru the cavern and came up near Sunflower Utah. But the locals are saying that they saw a UOF apired just before the lake appeared.

David walked outside Blue eyes did you hear that the lake repaired. Up in Utah close to a town called Sunflower some two hundred miles away.

It's a hundred and fifty miles out of our search our aria. But we have friends close to there.

Well you may want to tell your friends that if Alice is there she might be disorientated like Dave was.

Ok thank you I'll get the word out.

Good luck if you need our help let me know David said as he walked back inside.

The next morning Washen said let's stop and see that Judge again I got some paper for him to sign.

Where did you get that, I had my secretary make them up and fax it to the motel office.

When the Judge saw then walks in his court room. He finished the case that he was working with then called them up.

When I saw you walk in I knew it was going to be something different.

Your honor this is Dave Beld they release him but now they won't give him his car back. I have petitioned for them to give the car back and pay any towing bill.

The Judge kind of laughed I like the part of they pay the entire tow bill. Bring it up here and I'll sign it.

Washen handed it to the Bailiff who took it to the Judge who sign it. Then said you will keep me informed how all of this turns out

Yes your honor and thank you. Turning to Dave lets go get your car.

At the main gate of the US Army Proving Grounds Washen walk up and requested MR. Beld car.

Again the guard got on the phone and again up came the jeep with the man in charge.

Washen demanded for him to produce the car.

We don't have the car it is at the tow company.

Washen handed him the petition. This is a court order for you to return the car and you are to pay all towing charges. Now you have one hour to get the car in the same condition you pick it up or I will be talking to the Judge in two hours and Mr. Beld will be driving a new car and you people will be in court explaining why.

Waite here I will be right back.

A few minutes another jeep show up and a different soldier walked over to David, Alocla, Washen, and Mr. Beld we have a problem you see your car has been exposed to radiation above a safety limit.

So you are telling us that it was a UfO that took the water from the lake and while doing it contaminated his car.

NO I'm not saying that.

Then what are you saying it got contaminated in your custody. I would suggest you go get him a new car before this story gets to the news media.

There is no need to threaten us.

Oh that no threat I have Bear News on speed, diel as he held up his phone you do know Ted Donaldson.

Yes I know of him. We will get Mr. Beld car.

But you said it was unsafe do to radiation.

No I just said that to see what you would say.

Well now you know go get the man's car.

He walked over to the guard shack go get MR. Beld car it is in motor pool.

When they show up with MR. Beld car he went over and checks it out. Then waved to David and Alocla then told Washen thank you and took his card said be see you all around.

Washen turn to David if there nothing else I'll be heading back to the office. See you later when you think up something else and you need a lawyer for. Which way are you two going?

I think we need to go up north and see where all that water ended up.

David and Alocla were back in their motor home.

We found Alice she was pick up when the aliens were stealing the water and Alice got suck up but it sound like she cause so much trouble they dump the water.

You know one of these days the government is going to tell the truth to the people and they have making up stories for so long that nobody will believe them if they tell the truth this is a new one. A subterranean channel moves all that water and twenty people saw ET flying around.

CHAPTER 33

The BOLO

David and Alocla had parked their motor home and David was fishing Alocla set next to him.

I love Montana it so pretty with all its lakes everywhere.

Yes in the summer, nice if you have a snowmobile and a warm coat in the winter.

David and Alocla both jump up and turn around. Where hell did you come from, better yet how the hell did you find us?

Had a BNLO out for you agent Swan said and some state patrolman saw your license plate thought it was stolen till he called it in and was about to arrest you till they told him it was an Arizona plate not Washington plate with the same numbers and letters 375FLY but had a Bolo for it and if seen to call me.

Well son-of –a- bitch we have only been here for maybe an hour and a half what were you park around the corner.

What is BOLO Alocla asked?

It's what they do to find criminals.

But were not criminals are we Alocla asked.

NO the only thing criminal around here is Mr. Swan using a BOLO to fine us.

What dose BOLO mean she asked next?

It tells all law enforce to BE ON LOOK OUT for something in this case it was us.

Why was it on the lookout for us?

I don't know ask Mr. FBI over there, and how he got here so fast.

I took a plane to Kalispell and rented that car. As for being here have you seen the news?

No we don't watch the news it' all bad, if they had some good news it might be worth watching.

Well it's about Chicago they had nine murders.

See all bad news hell they have that on a slow weekend.

Let me finish done by the same person or person's three men and six women raped the woman but leaves the same trade mark an upside down cross on their chest. Here look at these pictures as he handed them to David. I don't think you should show them to Alocla their sickening.

Holey shit David said holding throwing up.

Let me see it,

No you really don't want to see this.

Yes I do come on show me.

David picked out the least gorse one and handed it to her.

She looked at it; Oh put her hand over her mouth and went to the nearest bushes and throwing up, coming back wiping her mouth.

I told you that you didn't want to see it

That's horrible why you let me see it.

You were determent to see it and that was not the worse one.

Oh putting her hand over her mouth again and going to the bushes.

So what do you want us to do?

Not we Mr. Swan said just you. His last victim a Linda Sarba after they try to revive her was talking to someone unseen to everybody. You know what I mean and said there were two of them and one was taken pictures and please don't let anyone see them please then she died. They tried to revive her but to no use.

The FBI has no ideal of who they are but we do think that there are two of them now working together. One serial killer is hard to find but two imposable. We need your special knowledge or special connection. So I need you to come with me.

Oh no where I go she goes pointing at Alocla'

Ok come on I have a plane waiting. I'll have the state patrol watch your bus.

It's a motor home.

Why don't you buy a real motor home .I'm sure you can afford one.

Have you ever seen gypsy's hippie's ride around in one of those fancy motor homes. If I could find one, we would be pulling a VW van around behind us. With flowers painted on it would make it easier for you to find us. So you would not have to call out every law enforce in the country. What if they came up and they tried to arrest us and I shoot one of them.

I did say do not attempt to arrest them in the BOLO to just call me.

What if some young rookie wants to make a name for himself and is lying face down in the dirt dead or worse yet Alocla and me are lying face down in the dirt handcuffed and you taking your time to get to the rookie oh you just wanted to talk to us.

Boy you are still mad about me putting out a BOLO on you.

Hell yes I went four years at that aria 54 and no one looked for me. Now every cop in the United States is looking for us and keeping you inform at where are at.

At the airport they pulled up next to the plane Alocla look at it so that an airplane.

It's a jet a lot faster than an airplane. Then David remembering Alocla had never been on an airplane. He reach for her hand it like a bird flying above the clouds, come on once you get used to it will be fun I'll hold your hand there's nothing to be scared of. David help her up the stairs and found her a seat then sat next to her holding her hand, when they started moving she squeeze it even tighter but when the plane lifted off the ground she really squeeze his hand. He had to pry her hand off of his. Its ok you can relax as he open and close his hand several times just to make sure they still worked. Take three deep breaths as he did and she follow suit. Now look out the window this is what the birds get to see.

Oh it is beautiful after that Alocla spent the rest of the trip looking out the window and everything was fine till she saw the ground coming up then the plane touch down and it was to squeezing the blood out of his hand again.

While in the air David went into the restroom.

What are we doing here?

We are going to try and find a serial killer with the help of your friends your friend who watch over Linda Sabre talked to her and she answered and said there were two of them and one took pictures and her last request don't let anyone see them so we are going to make sure that the only part of these picture is the face of the killers.

OK I'll go see what I can find out Linda Sabre Chicago recent passed.

David left and went back to the seat next to agent Swan. Tell me more about this Linda Sabre.

Well she was the latest victim and when she went flat line and they revived her she was talking to someone and mention that there were two people involve.

They were pick up at the airport and while in the car.

David are you there?

David heard this in his head yes he answered.

OK I got three of my friends.

Can they describe these attacker? And there were two people right.

Yes two men

Ok when we get some place we will get a sachet artist they can see the picture and tell me what to describe'

You think that will work?

Well I hope so. Swan did you follow this.

You need a sketch artist and a room all alone. And that there were two men we will get you set up a soon as we get to the office.

Once at the office Swan had it set up in a room the artist David and three misty figures that only David could see.

One had a young face one was older.

David repeated it to the sketch artist.

The young one had fairly long hair the other had like a crew cut.

David repeated.

The sketch artist stop them lets work on one at a time stick with the older one first older one had along face not round unshaven three or four days, short hair a little longer part down the middle eye brow a little bushy a little higher up.

Aright here are picture of noses the artist said as the screen showed Twenty-five different noses. Second row third from the right David heard so he pointed to it over one more David pointer at the one indicated yes that one the artist added it to the picture

Next the mouths as pictures of twenty mouths show up.

Three down four from the right

David heard and pointed yes he heard the artist add to the picture down just a little ears a little lower.

That's it we all agree that this matches what they saw.

They all agree David repeated.

Ok the younger one not really long but not round. Short but long on the chin, stock cap.

ok here are picture of eyes two from the bottom four from the right David pointed yes the artist add then full eyebrows just below the stocking cap not that full.

Ok now the noses as the picture show up

Two rows up fifth from the right, no more like two down third from the left.

There thinking between two different David inform the artist

Well we can put them on then change to the other

Frist one up two fifth from the right and two Down and three from the left

Ok here is the first one then a minute later here is the second.

Ok they agree the first one
And thin may 5 feet 9 in tall.
Yes that looks just like him, she is good.
They say that it looks just like him and you are a very good artist.
All right I'll get these two pictures to Mr. Swam. These are from you, not three people who are in this room with us right?
Got it, I wouldn't believe anything else.
David follows the sketch artist and she handed the sketch pictures to MR. Swan who took them to a computer and it started its search. The picture came up with a possible name and the picture sure was close. The computer keep scanning but never came up with the younger one. Swan turn to the people sitting in the office. OK here is our guy Jean Hambe fined his address and pass this picture around put out a bolo.
They did that to us Alocla said watching all the time this was taken place.
OK I got an address one of the agent said.
Good let go, remember this guy is dangers.
Eight agents headed toward the door. David followed.
Swam stop him where do you think you are going.
With you, are deal is if you find the camera and found the picture of Linda Sarba would not be seen and I'm going with you to make sure you stick to our deal.
I don't remember any deal like that.
I do it was made as a last wish, and I have three people you cannot see. Who want to honor that last wish?
Ok but you stay out of the way like stay in the car out of the way.
Yes OK.
Seriously you stay in the car.
OK and she going too.
Oh Jesus.
Yes he is listening to you along with three of his Angels.
Sorry as he looks around ok, get in the car.

They went to the address and like on television. They line up and single file they surrounded the door and did not knock just broke down the door and rushed in.

David did not stay in the car but follow them right in.

When they found a room full of really gross picture David asked anyone, meaning the three Guardian Angel which picture was Linda Sarbe . He could see a mist over by the pictures.

She not here.

David turned around and walk back to the car. When he sat down they came screaming in his head

The man in the picture is walking by right there.

David look up it was Jean Humbe he pulled out his phone and touches the number mark FBI. Finely Agent Swan answered .David blurted out Jean Humbe is coming in the building.

Unseen by David and Alocla who were sitting in the car eight FBI Agents spread out two went down the stairs, two went around the corner and two stood by the elevator the rest step back in the room

As Jean Humbe walk up to his apartment building he look around and saw all the same type of cars and all the same color. He looked around and then walked right pass the entrance to the building.

David still holding the phone yelled into it. He is suspicious and just walk on by David said.

Second later agents came running out of the apartment building. David jump out of the car and pointed at the man and yelled that him right there the man turned and look at David then to the men running toward him he started to run but the agents caught him in less than a block.

Faster than you can say Rumpelstiltskin they had him in the back of a car and everyone was leaving for the FBI office.

In some interrogation room they were trying to find out who and where his partner was.

But jean wasn't talking just asking for a lawyer.

David stood at the window watching this. When he said he wanted a lawyer the FBI could not question him anymore. David got up and walked in to the room. Are you question this man without an attorney then he handed Jean Washen card have you told them anything,

No.

Good alright now turning to Mr. Swan Jean here did not do anything it was all the kid what his name looking at Jean.

Jerry, Jerry Cook.

Yes Jerry Cook he was the one who did it. Jean only took pictures because Jerry said if he didn't go along that he would kill him that why he put that picture in his room and that Jerry had more pictures at his place. Isn't that right Jean?

Yes Jean answered.

Where is this place where Jerry keeps these other pictures? Swan asked?

Jean looked at David. David could see that had change Jean and put him on the defense.

Now wait Mr. FBI what is my man going to get out of this if he tell you where Jerry is at. No I'll tell you Jean here is innocent by way of o associations if he tells you where Jerry is he should get some compensation like he get off with probation for a year. You can see he really did have nothing to do with it.

Ok you win we recommend probation. Where is he?

Jean look at David and David just nodded his head it ok I got you covered.

Ok he lives over at Orland Park on 12th big brick building on the corner room 243.

Ok David said as he walks out.

Hay you are my lawyer

I never said I was a layer I just gave you a card of a friend of mine he the lawyer David walk out of the room.

Mr. Swam got up and went out, kind of laughed I would not have believed it if I didn't see it Lawyer David.

I never said I was a lawyer; now let's find this Jerry and those pictures and the deal is no one sees the pictures of Linda Sarba.

OK you go with us and you block off any thing you see inappropriate.

Swan got the agents together .I want two of you to stake out the building and tell us when this jerry guy is hone all we have is the sketch to go by. So be on the lookout and no one goes in till you have back up that means you call me.

An hour later Swan get a call this is Henderson Jerry cook is home right now.

Keep a watch on it we will be there in an hour. Alright everyone let's move the suspect is home. Ok David here your chance to get those pictures, but she stay here, pointing at Alocla.

Alocla started to protest.

Swan stop her no we know nothing about this Jerry Cook this is different Jean Humbe he had a record all petty crimes. I didn't see much danger, this guy we know nothing about that make him very dangerous. You are staying here.

So eight agent's line up outside Jerry cooks apartment Mr. Swan knock on the door FBI Jerry come out.

The answer came with a shot gun blast coming thru the door. The buck shot missed the agents but the flying wood from the door Hit Swan in the side knocking him to the floor. Three agents open fired thru the outside of the door then one of the agent hit the door with the battering ram and the agents rush in only to find Jerry laying on the floor dead with six bullet holes in him.

When the agents look around Jerry had a wall full of pictures David walked over to it which picture is Linda Sarba he asks nobody that the agents could see.

A mist went over to the wall as if to study it. Then floated back dear GOD these picture are horrible these animals. But Linda is not here.

What? Then David saw the camera sitting on the night stand. He went over and picks it up, and scan thru the pictures holding the camera up for someone to see if they were behind him.

Yes that's Linda Sarba.

What are you doing with that don't touch anything this is a crime scene an agent scolded him.

David push deletes all; there nothing on it I was sure that we would find some more pictures. But looking at that wall you can see both Dean and Jerry were involved with this rape and killing spree.

Thank you. That was Linda now she can move on.

Your welcome just glad I could help.

You are not helping touching everything on this crime scene so why don't you get out of here.

OK OK I'll just go and check on Mr. Swan as David left the room and found Swan. How are you doing buddy.

Oh I'm fine just a scratch they are making a big deal out of it, you find the pictures.

They were not on the wall but I found then in the camera and deleted them all.

What we may need them for a case against those two criminal's.

Oh there enough on that wall to make sure that they will never see freedom ever. And personally if anyone of them that is pictured on that wall was my daughter they would not even make it to jail. So there is no hard feelings about Jerry lying on the floor in there and as it goes Jean should be laying with him.

I know what you mean but, it is our job to bring a criminal or criminals to justice.

Well you still have to get us back to our motor home in Montana.

No problem I want that imitation Lawyer a long way from Jean Humbe then he laughed. I'm going to remember for a long time. On the other hand I didn't see anything.

CHAPTER 34

A short story

David and Alocla were sun bathing on a stretch of beach on Catalina Island When all of a sudden a boat load of people show up. David and Alocla decided to move to a more privet much smaller beach jest over the hill. On the way up the hill they ran into a bee nest. David step backward and trip then sat in a cactus patch since he was not wearing shorts he receive a butt full of needles. Given up the ideal of finding another beach they settle for a secluded cove. While he was bent over with Alocla pulling the cactus needles out of his back side.

He saw a small boat come around the corner and two girls jump out and were snorkeling in to shore. Meanwhile the two men brought the boat into the beach.

Are you David?

David looked around see nothing and it was not the voice of his sparkling blue eyed Guardian Angel. Yes he answered who are you?

Someone who needs your help see the girls floating out there she is in my charge and needs your help. One of them is not swimming, she is drowning.

David look out one was walking up to shore. The other one was floating face down with no snorkel. David jump up and grab his shorts and started running toward the water trying to put on the shorts falling down then rolling in the sand half way to the water coming up finishing pulling up the shorts, he ran as far as he could in the water. Then diving in and swimming out to the floating girl grabbing and turning her over and struggling to get her to the shore as he walk out and on the sand laying her down. Out of breath he asked does anyone know CPR the only response was her husband reach down and pulled her bathing suit up to cover her bear breast. David dug back in his mind he knew how to do this he had learn it in Boy Scouts a long time back but it came to him like he had learn it yesterday. 30 compression and two breaths Out of breath David began. On his third time of giving her the two Breaths, She coughs while he was giving them to her. David spit out the salt water and rolled her over on her side. She was back from the dead but not like in the movies. But like in real life she just laid there taken deep breaths. A minute or two later, a helicopters landed. David hadn't notice it before someone must had a least called the Coast Guard. They came over and took charge giving her oxygen. Then put her on a gurney and took it to the helicopter and flew her to the hospital.

David took Alocla hand and they walked back to their little cove David heard.

You are a Guardian Angel what they say about is right.

I don't know about the Guardian Angel but did you see that the hero running down the beach tearing off his shirt, running in the freezing water and saving the girl, and then bring her back to life.

NO Alocla said I saw what everyone saw was some wild man bare butt necked running down the beach falling down rolling in the sand then running into the ocean and finding A girl dragging her to shore, beating on her chest and trying to kiss her till she spit in his mouth. Then you rolled her over and she could throw up.

Boy Karen that was close it a good thing you were here and having a living charge. Who can hear us, how did it happen?

We think when he was in Alaska and got a shock with 440 volts and lived. It spark the brain cells like it dose with a defibrillator. But unlike a defibrillator it last longer. We were sure lucky, we have heard of some of the things he has been doing with your help and he is good looking too.

Ladies I can hear you and when you let me I see the misty form you take.

Oh shit.

From then on David did not hear them talking about him.

CHAPTER 35

Nancy

Alocla and David were heading up to Como from San Diego.

Stop David there a lady lying in the ditch just up ahead.

David stopped the car and walked up the road a ways then found the lady badly beaten and he notice her arm turn wrong he try to move it and she let out a scream Alocla came up

See if you can help her I bring up the motor home and will try to get her to the hospital. Alocla stayed with her and David went and got the motor home then help get the lady into the motor and drove to the nearest hospital. It wasn't hard to get check in she had been there several times.

Nancy I keep telling you to leave that man one of these days he will kill you,

It looks like you know the nurse told her as she took her in the back to get her arm fix. Where does she live?

Up the road a bit old house with some old cars and a jack up pick up in the yard? Her husband is a no good drunk beats her up once a month.

Why doesn't she leave him?

She has twice he just finds her and beats her up worse each time

Alocla why you stay here with Nancy for a bit I'll be right back.

What are you going to do? David heard in his head, just go for a little ride.

The nurse look at David if that ride is where I think you are going you better take a gun Harlam is a big man.

David just shrugs it off and went out and unhooked the jeep from the back of the motor home. Pull it around next to the motor home and went in, then shortly came out and got in the jeep and drove away. He drove till he found the house the nurse describes right down to the jack up pickup in the yard. David knocks on the door with his left hand in his right he held a baseball bat hidden by the outside door jam.

A man six inches taller than David answer the door David could smell the booze on his breath,

What do you want?

We just took your wife to the hospital badly beaten and a broken arm.

So the bitch fell down what do you want me to do about it.

You probably want to go see her.

Tell the bitch to call a cab when she gets out.

Wrong answer David switch the bat to both hands and swing as hard as he can hitting the man on the side of the knee dropping the man to the floor as Harlam put his arm out to push himself up David swung the bat again this time hitting between the elbow and wrist the bone shedder the bone that was once straight look like the letter L. the defenseless man look up as David swung again stopping inches from the side of his face.

If you hurt my sister again, I will come back here with a gun and blow both of your Knee off and my gun it a 44 magnum so it will probably take your lag off from the knee down and you will never know when I will be coming. Now you can call 911 and get a ride to see my sister your wife at the hospital. That is if you can crawl over to that phone over there. Remember I will be watching you. With that David swung the bat again this time coming in contact with the Harlam ribs cracking two of them. David turned and walk out the door and got in his car went back to the hospital hook it back up behind the motor home Went in and handed the nurse one of Washen cards if Nancy ever come back in here again call the number on this card and we will handle it . Taken Alocla hand walks out to the motor home/ bus and they went on their way to Como.

Down the road Alocla look over at David I didn't know that you had business cards.

I don't I gave her Washen.

David heard laughing from three different people in his head.

We never thought that is what you were up too

CHAPTER 36

OIL

David and Alocla arrived at Como. They noticed a new building at the other side of town with a tower coming out the top. David found Griz and asked about the building.

Oh that's Hime he is drilling for oil it a new way he invented.

David turned to Alocla, Hime I don't place him.

He is the boy who could throw the rock and hit the camera in compound two.

He went to collage for engineering Griz said he wanted to go to space like Krima will be doing. But then he got more out of geology and when Jason Simmons try to burn down Como because he thought there was oil under it. Hime got into that and invented a new way of drilling for it.

I think we should go over and congratulate our young genius. Heck I want to see this anyway David said heading over to the new building.

As they entered the building they were met by Hime. Alocla it is good to see you and you to David.

I hear you are a roughneck now David said.

Roughneck Hime repeated looking at David?

That is what they call oil field worker.

I know that but no one around here does. Have you work in the oil field.

Yes I have spent a little time working on an oil derrick.

This is a little different type of drilling I'm using laser to drill.

What? what happens when you hit oil or even a gas pocket.

That's the great part I have figure out a way that it works backwards, from the laser that everyone knows. It works making it cold crushing the rock and brings it out. See that rock coming out it is cold and broken up basically making a perfect hole to any size we want then we drop a casing in till we hit oil.

That sound interesting is it working.

We are down five hundred and thirty seven feet. In less than twelve days. And we are with in twenty feet of a large oil reservoir. We slow down the drilling so that we will hit tomorrow morning and celebrate then, so you are just in time.

Damn this is sure different than when I was working in the oil fields.

Oh it is a lot different now we won't need cement or to have to perforate the casing. We won't need a pump we are going to push warm water into the well from the warm springs over there over at the other new building and floating the oil up to just a small pump to the tank that we don't have yet. When we get it all working chevron will buy all the oil and part of the deal is we get to set the price of the fuel at the pump and they want to buy the paten for the drilling method and they are talking nine figure numbers closer to ten figures we are letting Washen handling it.

It sure look like you have got things going your way Alocla told him.

If you mean from living in a cave to a castle on the hill thank you David.

Don't thank me you people did all of this on your own. I'm going to check out that hot springs.

Don't be so modest. Like he said they would still be living in caves if it weren't for you, I knew when he said hot springs your eyes lit up. After all the hot springs you have been to. Now you got your own, and I suppose it going to be clothing optional.

You damn right at least half of it.

Who is he talking to Hime asked Alocla?

Oh he has a habit of talking to himself he calls it his Guardian Angel. Basically I think it talking to the other side of his head, they both laughed.

The next day almost all of the Como family was out to watch the last foot to be drilled. Hime was the center of attrition he checks the shut off value he went over and flip the switch and nothing happen. Hime went over to the control box when he opens the door he could tell right away that one of the pressor was missing. Hime look at it in disbelief. Standing there he just shook his head as David walk over.

Everything OK?

No, one of the control is missing if they would have taken the one next to it would be the forward laser. And this place would just be a hole in the ground.

Who knows what control the laser?

Only me and a few technician because if someone wanted to destroy this project he would take the other one it was one of a kind. It is the main brain just the technology alone is worth the millions they were going to pay and now they got it and if they have anyone intelligent enough to read it. It will take me a week to build another one. Did anyone see someone around this equipment last night? I need to contact the sheriff to keep an eye on this.

I'll do you one better I'll call a friend in the FBI.

David went and got his damn smart phone as he called it. And scroll down to the one Saying FBI and tap the little phone next to it.

Well hello David what's on your mind?

Mr. Sawn we are having some thief trouble out here at Como. I was hoping you could help us fine a major component out of the main control of the drilling machine.

I have heard that one of the genies friends invented a well drilling machine. That will revelation the way we drill for oil also you were giving a Demonstration at Como.

We were till this part turn up missing.

I'm in D.C. but I will have a local agent stop by.

An hour later a car pulls in and the man got out and asked for David.

The one he asked look around then pointed that him over there, the men walked up to David are the one in charge around here. No but I'm David who oversee everything.

You're the one I don't know who you are but I do know that you are important. D.C. called me and said to drop everything and get out here immediately and they would have a supervisor out here in two hours. What is going on?

Come over her this is Hime he is in charge of this plant and we are missing a part that if we don't find could blow up this whole town. Then David wink at Hime. Hime this man is from the F.B.I tell him what is missing.

Hime had caught the wink Ok right over here as he headed over to the control panel. David walked away toward the hot springs.

Is it true this Whole place will blow up; I have a lot of friends around here?

Well hi bright blue eyes how many friends do you have around here I have not heard anyone else but you just now.

That is because nothing was directed to you. As for how many, everyone who came from arisa 55 has one.

Then you can help us was it anyone from the camp who took the controls.

No it had to be from outside Como. Whoever is it is a very bad person because they are do not have a Guardian Angel and we know which way they will be going if they die.

Can you look around out there and find something.

David walked to where there were three pipes coming out of the ground with hot wat coming out of them almost two feet hi.

They were coming together to make a small stream about fifty feet long before soaking back in the ground.

Oh I love seeing your mind trying to figure out you are going to make that hot spring your play pen.

If you can see my mine you see a big family pool over here as he pointed in one direction and clothing optional over here and a holding pool over here for the oil well.

Do you think the board will go for it?

People travel thousands of miles to soak in a hot Spring.

David next thing was to call Washen how much of this air base do we own David asked?

The people of Como have been buying up everything as a cording to our agreement with the government. We now own all of the two hundred and thirty five thousand acers. Half of that is only worth two dollars an acer but now that Hime found oil under it make it worth a lot more.

Next David went over to

Hime how long till you are ready to go.

AsIf we don't fine the original, I could do it in at least a week.

Alocla and I will be gone for a week hope to be back by then. Going and getting Alocla want to go for a ride.

Ok where are we going?

Going to check out a few hot springs.

We're not taking the motor home?

No we are taken the jeep and a tent.

Alright camp out under the stars.

The first place they went was Beale hot spring was a little crowded but David and Alocla spent a day socking in the spring and taken picture that night camp out under the stars feeling well rested and relaxing. The next day they went Alanta hot spring where they found a place that was clothing optional David got permission to take picture as long as it didn't show personal body part, one lady said no so David did not include her in the picture the rest didn't mind. They again camp out because they sock in the water till way after dark and the stars were out while they sat in the warm water. The next they drove to Hesperia California stay that night in a motel then the next day went up to the Boden Ranch park the car and hike down to the hot spring they came on a river and on the other side were three hot pools, the first was shallow and real hot second one up was warmer and deeper next to

It a little high up was the big deep pool just right temperature now out of either pool you could get up and dive in the cold river and swim upstream fifteen feet to a hot water shower water falling twenty. The whole hot Springs was all clothing optional David took picture with people permission mainly of the river and the hot spring on the other side and their deferent elevations

You were not supposed to spend the night but several people did after dark David and Alocla stayed all night setting up their tent at night so they spent most of the night in the hot spring with stars above and no lights to making the star even brighter and see more star than ever.

David and Alocla left around noon and hike back up to their car at the ranch and stay that night in a motel in the morning drove back to Como. At Como David found Hime how is it going?

I'm just about done building the new component been working day and night, should be ready tomorrow at lease to test. The FBI had a lead on who stole the first one but they never got it back.

David went out and found Griz. Hay buddy think you can get the board together tomorrow.

Sure what you got in mind?

You see that hot water coming out of the ground here I've been thinking of putting it to use by building some pools and have the tourist attraction with a hot springs and bring in more people and put Como on the map.

That night David printed off the picture off with the help of the lady in the office.

The next morning Griz had got the board together and did pitch his hot spring set up and show them the picture.

Then at noon Hima was ready to drill the last foot of the well, most of the people who live in Como were there. At high noon

Hima hit the switch and the reverse laser came on and two minute later the crude oil started up the well when the first shot hit the top and went ten feet in the air when the automatic value close but not before letting a small amount get out and it was enough to get the crowed showered with crude oil like they had seen on television. A cheer went up from the crowed. They had their oil well.

CHAPTER 37

Sink or swim

*A*re you David?
David slowly looks around this was not the voice of his guardian Angel.
Yes who are you?
See that young lady over to your right under the umbrella She is my charge and she is thinking about ending her life. Her boyfriend drops her for her best friend. And she is planning to just walk out into the water; she does not know how to swim. Oh no there she goes. Can you help me please?
David still not sure what was going on got up and walk toward the girl, who was at the edge of the water.
Do you really think it is worth it?
The girl stopped, are you talking to me?
Yes you look like someone who was about to do something very stupid.
How do you know what I'm about to do.
Because I have been in your situation, my wife left me for another man. And I thought it was the end of the world. And by killing myself would make me feel better. I even went to the tallest building in the city twenty two stories up as I climb out of the window and looked down at the street and I thought this will make her happy. Yes it would well why I would want to make

her happy. After she had did this to me. No there a lot of better women in this world who would not do this to a man she was supposed to love. It must not have been real love in the first place. I climb back in that window and went on with life and the next day I meet Alocla. I was not looking for love but it found me. I don't know what happen to you but I do know that whatever it is you are stronger than that. Out there is your Guardian Angel watching over you and plans for your life, and it does not include going out in the water and ending it. So what can be so bad you would end it all?

My boyfriend HA, all he wanted was to get me to sleep with him and when I did he laugh at me and said I just won the bet. I didn't understand but the next day he was kissing my best friend and would not talk to me, that when I understood the, I won the bet.

Well he sounds like the scum of the earth. Instead of making him happy with his conquest why not make him pay for what he did.

How do we do that?

There are several ways how old is this boy.

Nineteen

And how old are you seventeen.

That is one way of getting even with him have sex with a minor is illegal you could put him in jail. That is one way or you could tell your girl friends that you were right he wasn't worth a shit less than minuet it was over.

That would get him, she smiled.

I saw that smile see life is getting better. I'm also sure that you have a Guardian Angel watching over you and you will find the right guy who will love you for more than your body and I have this feeling it will be for your brain and personality. You give me one minute and I bet I can find more of your great qualities. Looking at her then looking all around.

Got that, straight A student. She Plays on the girl basketball team, and on the debate team.

You're a straight A student you play a sport say Basketball, and I'll bet you are great debate so you're on a debate team, right.

A Road You Don't Want to Travel

How do you know all that about me?

Well just talking to you I can tell you are smart so in school you would get good grades. Your body is in good shape and you are tall so that basketball, and you use the right words that debate and your Guardian Angel told me so. See I told you that you have a Guardian Angel. A girl with all of that going for you, you would be the catch of a life time and if I hadn't met my soulmate I would be looking for a girl like you.

You had better straighten that out.

And speaking of that great person and soulmate here she is Alocla this is oh sorry didn't get your name.

Laraita

Well Larita meet the love of my life then he (smiled at Alocla) Alocla.

How do you do you're not going out for a swim in that dress are you?

No I'm going home and get even with a guy I thought I loved as she turned and walk up the sand back to the road.

Alocla turned to David you still have one of Washen cards?

Yes and reach in his pocket and handed it to her.

Alocla caught up with Laraita you ever need a friend call this number and ask for Alocla I'll will be there.

Back down on the shore with David I got most of that. Do you really think she was going to kill herself and how did you know her.

Her guardian Angel told me.

And this Angel told you she played sports and is a good student and that she was about to end life by going into the ocean

David just smiled and said yes.

You know so much has happen that I'm starting to believe in your Guardian Angel.

Oh you have one too you just don't know how to listen to her.

Are all guardian women?

David heard laughing that no one elce heard.

Why does the living believe an Angel had to be a woman? Some are men some can be a dog or any pet,

Everyone is different I knew one that was a teddy bear to a small child.

A teddy bear you're making this up. Teddy bears don't talk.

They do if they are assigning as a guardian Angel.

CHAPTER 38

A goodwill mission

David and Alocla had just pulled into the camp ground for the night and were just settling in when David heard.
 David how would like to do some good neighbor friendship. See that camper two spot down his name is Sam Loaden he just lost his wife to cancer a week ago and is kind of lost doesn't really have any friends.

Ok tell me a little about him..

He was married for 32 years. Work as a truck driver for 25 years finely retired one year ago. Because his wife had cancer, lasted a year then she passed and he has just been going here and there kind of lost.

Where is he from, where did he live?

Why?

I need something to talk about; I can't just walk and start talking about anything. Does he drink alcohol? Come on give me some to work with?

Let me guess you're talking with your Guardian Angel and were about to get into more trouble I thought they were to keep you out of trouble

Alocla said as she was looking at him.

No this is a good will mission on our neighbor down there pointing to the camper down the way. He needs a shoulder to lean on.

So how are you supposed to help?

I don't know but obviously someone does David said looking around.

Well if your Angel told you so, I guess you better do it. Don't want her to be mad.

David laughed I'm going to take a walk and he headed toward Loaden's camper.

Found him sitting at the table outside of his camper with his hands covering his face and a drink sitting on the table in front of him.

I would think you're a truck driver who just ran out of driving time and you're only a hundred miles from home or someone who is thinking way too hard.

Sam looked up, both he said.

Hi I'm David and been there more than once myself.

Oh hi Sam Loaden he said as he stood up reaching out his hand as a hand shake.

David accepted it and ask who you drive for?

Landwick Transport.

Oh a car hauler, I was with DeYoung"s Refrigeration, refer hauler then went independent. Fuel got to expensive and the freight prices never went up.

Yak I know, can I offer you a drink?

Sure what you got?

Captain and coke.

OK that what I usually have Captain and root beer.

Well that does sound good I'll have to try it out.

Then tomorrow happy hour is on me.

Are you in the bus down there pointing at David bus?

Yes we have converted it over to a motor home that way we got the lay out we wanted. Do you play pool they have a pool table down at the club house?

Some but I'm not very good that it.
Good either I'm I.
Sam grabs his bottle of captain and the large coke.
The next morning David sat up in bed at around 10: o'clock holding his head.
It look like you cheer him up Alocla said handing David a wet cold towel for his head you two were singing and telling trucker stories having a hell of a good time. It was good to see you laughing and relaxing for once.
I can tell you he sure can drink and like fishing.
So you do have something in common.
The next day in the afternoon Sam came over to David and Alocla.
Are you ready to try Captain and root beer David asked?
After last night I think I well wait a day.
I know what you mean; Alocla said we were having a good time singing karaoke by our self. It felt good to unwind, till this morning how about a plain Pepsi.
That sounds good. I don't remember unwinding like that since my wife die thank you.
I was thinking of calling a friend up in Ilwaco
Washington who owns a fishing charter and it should be salmon season and if it is, you want to go?
Now that sounds like something I have not done in a long time, yes I'm in for that.
I" call my friend tonight and find out.
For the next two hour David and Sam spent telling fish and trucker stories. But Sam did mention how he uses to spend a lot of time fishing with his sons Larry and Sandy.
That night David called his friend up in Ilwaco.
And found out the Salmon were out in the ocean. That he would have room on the boat next Sunday.
When David hung up the phone He sat back, hay blue eyes are you out there?
Yes well you sure spread goodwill really good.

Good I hope you all remember that when I die and tell the BIG GUY all about it.

Oh the Big guy knows.

Can you and your friends find out where his sons Larry and Sandy are I want to invite them to a fishing trip with their father?

You are really carrying this a long way. I'll check might get a location but not a phone number she laughed,

David turned to Alocla do you want to go fishing in the ocean.

Yes you talk about it a lot. Like that a good lake for fishing, I'll bet there a big fish in that river but you never went, is this ocean fishing just a fun.

Oh yes the fish are a lot bigger, and more fun to catch and salmon smoked is the treat of a life time.

Alocla eyes got big, you smoke fish?

Not like a cigarette or pipe, it is slow cooked with smoke for heat.

Like we would dry our meat back at Como Alocla said.

Yes only they use Cherrie or apple wood.

Well we located Sandy Loaden in Amboy Washington, still looking for Larry. All we know is somewhere near Bremerton Washington.

Shell we see how lucky we can get and how smart phone is.

I knew you were talking to your quote unquote Guardian Angel. You have been looking out in space for the last five minutes.

Come on smart phone talk to me Sandy Loaden in Amboy Washington.

We have a Sandy and Tari Loaden in Amboy Washington. At 231 Youger lanes Phone number is 360-555-0908.

David pushed the little phone on his phone. He heard it ring once then twice then before the third ring someone answer.

Ya what are you selling I'm not buying and what you are giving away I probably already have bye.

Click.

No too late he already hung up. David pushed the little phone again. David One rings two rings and a pick up.

I said

A Road You Don't Want to Travel

Don't hang it is about your dad David yelled in the phone.

What did you say about my dad?

Hi my name is David I have met your dad here in the camp grounds and we are both retired truck drivers and he was lonely so we hit it off and found out, we both like fishing so a friend of mine in Ilwaco Washington has a charter boat business and said he would take us out salmon fishing .your dad told me how you and your brother Larry like to fish. So I talk my friend Bill to take us out Sunday and I thought it would be nice surprise to get you and Larry to come along won't cost you a thing what do you think want to go salmon fishing with your old man.

Hell yes is it alright to bring my wife Tari dad has never met her.

Sure I don't see any problem I think let me get back to you, by the way do you have Larry phone number, and I'd like to get him to go.

Just a minute honey you got Larry phone number.

Yes it's on my phone here it is, 360-502-6786 why?

Dad planning a fishing trip out of Ilwaco.

Do I get to go?

I'll see in the phone did you hear that.

I'll check should be alright. Call you tomorrow night.

All right call me tomorrow goodbye.

David diel the number Sandy gave him.

Hello this is Larry.

Yes this is about your dad I'm David and a friend of you dad and we are planning a fishing trip and would like.

I'm sleeping leave me a message you know what to do at the beep BEEP.

HI this David a friend of your dads and Sandy and I are planning a surprise fishing trip for your dad this Sunday and no cost to you we would like you to come along call me please 502-213-1890 David hung up. And was just setting it down when it rang startling so much he drop the phone. Picking it off the floor .Hello

You just call me about dad?

This must be Larry?

Yes what that about dad?

Yes I met him the other day and we got to talking about fishing and I have a friend who owns a fishing charter business in Ilwaco Washington and I have set up a charter Sunday as a surprise for your dad and he talk a lot about you and Sandy so I thought I would surprise him and have you two show up and go with us.

Wow good idea I haven't seen him in a year right after Mon died.

OK I' get the information and call you tomorrow.

David hung up then call bill his friend with the charter boat.

Hello Ilwaco sea charter this is Bill.

Hay Bill this is David again how many people can you take on your boat Sunday.

Morning or afternoon?

You know me when the best time to catch fish,

Boy you have been gone a long time if you forgot that.

Ok when is the incoming tide?

Around 11 o clock.

Ok morning.

How many

Say six or seven

You want the whole boat.

If you can arrange and not put you out,

Hell buddy IOU that much you help me out what three or four times.

I'm not collecting on those I came into some money and will pay full price and then a bonus if at least three people catch fish.

If you only catch three fish out of six or seven people. The ride is free. How big of a bonus.

Enough to pay for a day worth of fuel.

Ok buddy you are on, Sunday 6.00 am. Be on the dock.

Thanks buddy see you then, David hung up the phone.

Wow you would make a great Guardian Angel.

It was not a voice David had not heard before but it did sound familiar.

Like he said you would be a great Guardian Angel. No what I should say you are a great GOOD WILL AMBASSADOR.

This was David's blue eye Guardian angel.

All this time Alocla was sitting across the table watching him. Does thiis mean that we are going to go fishing with Sam and his kids? Who have not seen their father in a year? Is that what your Guardian Angel told you to do?

No they just asked me to be friends with him the rest I dream up to get him back to his kids.

Well that's sweet of you that probably is why I like so much.

Well if you like me so much how about we go to bed and you show me.

Getting up and taken his hand, I thought you would never ask.

An hour later they just laid there, Alocla said wow that was fantastic I'm going to have to give you a day of relaxing with the boys more often.

The next morning David went down to Sam's camper and told him of the planed fishing trip. That if they left these camp grounds at around noon they could set up in the parking lot in Ilwaco Saturday night then catch the boat at 6 o'clock in the morning.

David did not tell him about Larry and Sandy being there.

That night David called Larry and Sandy and told them of the plan. That he and their father would be there Saturday night.

Three days later David and Alocla pack up the camp site and Sam did the same. Then both headed north to Ilwaco. They set up next to each other at the back of the lot sitting in their chair talking and having a Captain and cream soda they had captain and root beer on Thursday. Now David broke out the cream soda to try. Alocla was having the half bottle of cream soda that David and Sam didn't use with their Captain Spice rum. When a voice behind Sam. said captain and cream soda never try that mind if try that it was a male voice.

Tari came around from behind carrying a glass and fixed a drink Sam looks a little surprise from where he was sitting he could not see Sandy but David and Alocla could see Sandy.

Tari fix a drink and drank it drank it and said this is great .My husband would like it, she hollow out Honey come over here and try this. Sam was taken a drink so he didn't see Sandy till he was all the way in front of them fixing a drink.

When Sam recognize Sandy he spit out what was in his mouth and drop the glass. He jump and gave him a big hug.

When Sam let him go Sandy turned to Tari. Dad this is my wife Tari. Sam went over and gave her a big hug it good to know you .I was sure my boy would never get married. Never could find the right girl.

Well we meet in school and then ten years later met and last year we got married.

Hay what is this having a family reunion and not inviting me as Larry walked into the light.

What both of you here now how can that be Sam went over to Larry and gave him a big hug.

Larry said when there a fishing trip I have to show you two how to catch them.

Sandy went over to David you must be David reaching his hand out, don't know how to thank you for this.

Just let me catch some of the fish. This is Alocla my girlfriend. Were just glad to get you and your brother and your father all back together for some fishing.

Sam came over you know about this, how did you do it it's like a miracle.

Not a miracle it was easy with the help of a few Guardian angels.

Are we still going fishing?

Hell yes David look at his watch tomorrow at 6 o'clock think I turn in you visit with your kids and I'll see you all at 5 in the morning. Going over to Alocla are you ready for bed.

She looks at David and smiled yes are you. He just took her hand headed to the Motor home.

The next morning at 6 o'clock they all were down on the dock when Bill walked up with his deck hand. Well David long time no see what have you been doing these last few years.

If I tell you, you would not believe me?

You remember the bonus then he laugh it just good to see you, let's get aboard this is my deck hand Lenny He will help you amateurs.

I don't think that were all armature except Alocla there she the only one who have never been fishing, ever.

Ever Bill repeated why is she hanging around with you. A looker like her could have anyone she wants or anything she wants.

She has that now besides she like my smile.

I don't think so come let's go catch some fish

Bill was true to his word everyone got their limit and Alocla got two after losing two she learn how to catch salmon with a no barb hook.

David paid for the trip tip the deck hand $200.00 and fill up the boat fuel tanks.

Bill told him he really did not need to when he heard the story about getting Sam reunited with his kids.

Sandy and Larry talk Sam to set up permanently at a RV park on Cranberry road near the ocean. And became a good friend of Bill and went out fishing every chance he could get.

David and Alocla would stop by when they were up that way when Alocla wanted to go fishing. And David needed a rest playing pool in the club house at the RV Park. And it always cost a bottle of Captain Spice rum and cream soda.

CHAPTER 39

The Earthquake

Alocla and David were on I 5 north that runs right thru the middle of Sacramento California when all of a sudden the motor home started wavering back and forth across the road. Damn a flat tire David said hang on as their motor home went into the ditch.

The problem was even though the bus was stop it was still shacking. Not a flat tire it was an earthquake happening. While they were sitting there watching building all around shake till all of a sudden they started falling down people running everywhere but with building all around there was nowhere save to run. Soon the ones, who could not get out of the way, were buried in piles of steel and concrete.

David sullen heard voice all around him. But the clearest one was his shinny Blue eye Guardian Angel.

David our friends have charges all over, who are still alive but are buried you need to help them.

What do you think I can do?

We can show you where they are and you can get help to get them out.

All of them some must be already be dead.

Yes the ones who have already have passed on and their Angels are gone to show them the way.

Ok where do we start?

My people will stand over where their charges are at we know that you can see us look.

David look out at twenty or more misty shapes standing over the pile of rubble that many?

Yes

David harried over to the closest one and yelled over to the people standing around everyone over here there someone buried right here as he started move concert off.

Other joined in and soon they had the man out the ambulance was going by one of the helper flag them down. Meanwhile David move to the next one and called out every one over here as he started moving more rubble as Alocla help him soon everyone was helping this time it was a lady. David went to where only he could see the Angel standing. Everyone come over here we have another one everyone came over and started move chunk of concrete and steel only this time the steel was too big by now a fire truck had showed up and the firemen were helping one of then got out the saw and the jaws of live and moved the steel beam. While two other people pulled the boy out.

David moved to the next one and called out over here. And started moving the rubble

One of the firemen walked over to him how is that you know where to look. David exhausted fell back to rest looked at him, I don't know it just these people seem like I walk up to a spot and the pulse in my hand start beating and become cold. David stood up and looks for another mist figure and walked over to it when he got to the same spot as the Angel he stopped here is another one. He started moving debris and in a short time had a foot uncovered. The firemen started moving the other debris with the help from the paramedic. They had the girl under covered and were help into the ambulance. The search went on into the night when the fire dept. put up light and more volunteers show up, and one had brought in a backhoe that help speed up but it meant to be more careful by midnight they had uncovered twelve people who were still alive. A few that weren't that they found dead while digging out the live ones.

Alocla had been making sandwiches

Handing out water that one of the volunteer had taken her to Safeway to pick up.

It was taken to long to dig out the live ones David had notice that every now and then a mist Angel would disappear. David guess the meaning, that person had died before they had got to them.

The volunteer were getting tired too. And the more they found the harder it was to find but David wasn't going to quite he marked a few more spot then sat down to rest.

You're doing great; you cannot give up now please.

Tell me did all of these people have Guardian Angels.

Not all did if they still live at home they were watched over by the Angel who watches over the mother or farther in a lot of cases both.

How many more are there are here?

Five more here, there are more than a hundred all over town and we are losing them fast.

How do you deal with death all the time and not be effective.

The people we are charge with are going to a better place you should see the smiles and happiness the joy they receive. They have No pain that they have live with for years.

How about the ones that don't have a Guardian Angel?

You don't want to hear about them.

They had been digging out people for twenty hour and there was only one marker left to check. There were more bodies but only one with an Angel standing over it.

All in all they had save nineteen people and fifteen had Angel standing over them. They had also uncovered another seven bodies.

They were digging out the last one David had said that there was someone alive when the Angel standing over the spot disappeared.

No no no David said we were so close.

It not your fault you did the best you could do.

But why only nineteen saved there were more people out there we saw them.

We lost three in the hospital. But don't worry they are still looking for people.

You save a lot of people to day and the only thing I can think of is that you have a photo memory and you saw where they were when the buildings started falling.

I never knew that I had a photo memory One of the paramedics came over to David you might not have known it before, maybe it is just because of the circumstance of the condition we have here, triggered it. Maybe but it sure save lives.

Alocla had been working at getting their motor home out of the ditch and arraign for a tow truck to do it. It was sitting by the edge of the road with. David walks over to it and checks the Damage it was all minable. David went in and lay down and was fast asleep dreamed of suffocating under concrete and steel. Then throw off the blankets from in front of his face breathing deeply. Telling himself it was only a dream, but he now knew what the people who had got buried had gone thru.

CHAPTER 40

Ammie

David do not say anything we have someone who needs your help. It's part of your family, Ammie she being held drug up and lock in a shad in Maywood California.

David got up and went outside. OK what are you talking about?

Your foster sister Ammie is being held by two men and have been prostituting her out they are keeping her drug up behind a gas station.

You say in May wood where is that?

It's a suburb of Los Angeles.

Ok I will run over and check it out. David went back in the motor home.

So what was that all about Alocla asked?

Oh nothing I have to run in to Los Angeles. For awhile

You are such a damn liar I have known for over five years and you cannot lie worth a shit.

You know you are getting quite a potty mouth.

I know what that means, and anything I say you said it first. I'll get the motor home ready to go.

You're not going this might get dangers.

So I was right you were talking to your Angels and they want something, I'm going as she started putting thing away making the motor home secure for travel. An hour later David and Alocla were in their motor home, and on their way to Maywood California.

Once there the found a place where homeless people had set up their camp and a few trailers one broke down motor home. How did they know it was broke down well the hood was up with four homeless super mechanic working on it or at lease trying to fixing it. Also the two flat tires really gave it away. David parked up the street, unhook the jeep. Walk over to the bus. Problem he asked? One super mechanic, yes the fuel pump out of it but it is way down there where we cannot see it.

That because these newer ones they put the fuel pump in the fuel tank and it is electric one.

One of the mechanic who looked, well definitely was half stone. And David was wondering about the other half didn't think these older motor home had the pump in the tank.

David didn't want to be a smart ass but he knew that the pump was in the tank because of the long way the fuel had to be pump from the back where most tanks are to the front where the motor is.(just a bit of trivia). Anyways these brain surgeons were not going to get the motor running. They figured that out too so they all went into the motor home and smoke some more marijuana, must have been good stuff to what I know about marijuana they cough there head off and it smelled like someone hit a skunk.

David went back to his motor home and told Alocla to watch the motor home he would be back shortly. She started to protest but David stay firm on this.

David drove around the block then pulled over Ok are you here talking to no one.

Yes David the gas station is over five blocks and up two it's a Mobil station what do you have plan.

Don't know just play it by ear will see. David drove to the station and was getting gas and a kid came out. David asked hay do you know if any of those homeless people over the other way do any hooking. I'm looking for a good one to rent for a while.

How much you want to pay.

I don't know forty or fifty bucks.

Tell you what fifty dollars I got a sister who does tricks out back.

Well this is my lucky day. Let's see what you got?

Just pull around back. How do I know you are not going to mug me?

No I'm just trying to get you laid and my sister fifty dollars It all business. My name is Skip and held out his fist for a fist bump.

Ok and fist bump him back. I'll meet you there David said then got in his jeep and pulled around back. Ok let's see what I'm paying for.

He went over to the shed and pull the lock off and open the door and there laid Annie on an old mattress naked and really space out she was not aware of anything around her.

This was more than David could take; he brought a hay maker around hitting Skip on the cheek just below the eye it was going to leave a black eye for sure. Skip got up and came at David David laid the second blow right in the middle of his gut when he bent over David grab the back of his collar and slam his head into the shed .

Skip staggered back what wrong with you he asked?

That just happens to be my foster sister Ammie. And she is going with me.

Well I'm going to get the police.

You do that while I get her dress. David found a pair of shorts and when he started the putting on the shirt. Ammie came a little coherent.

Ammie it is me David.

She open her eyes David I Love you, you take me home please.

Yes I will take you home.

Ammie through her arms around David I love you take me home.as she try to get up.

Hay you come out here.

David looked at the door there stood Skip and a much taller and bigger. David stood up and step outside Good you brought help now both of you get her in the back seat of my car.

What you little shit face she not going anywhere.

I told you nicely now both of you pick up Ammie and put her in the car as he reach behind him and pulled out his gun. Now I don't want to shoot you but I will and after seeing what you two are doing here I would not think twice about doing it. Now pick up Ammie and put her in the car.

Both of then turn around and help or more like drag her out and put her in the car.

Now take off your pants.

Why you some kind of a pervert.

No I just don't want you come after me and I have to shoot you. Your pants will be over by the building over there. Now get them off.

I'll shoot you in the knee and this being a 45 it would probably take your lag off with the knee. David then fired a shoot between them that went through the door of the shed and into the mattress.

It convinces then that David meant what he was saying. They both took off their pants.

Now get in the shed.

I' going to kill you the big one said.

Plenty of people who have said that before as David said he drove off. He zig zag a few block then got on the 405 till he found the sign saying hospital next exit he had seen it coming in it just took him some time to find it again.

At the hospital David pulled into the emergence and went to the door and got a nurse attrition who open the door

My sister they have been giving her drug and rape her.

The nurse yelled something back in the door and they came out with a gurney put Ammie on it and went back inside told David they needed to fill out some papers. Have you ever been to a hospital their ideal of some papers is the size if a ream of paper using both side. Unless you are a lawyer you really have no idea at what you are signing after filling out the paper work they tell you. That you can wait in the waiting room but Ammie would be out for a few days.

David was not going to stay at the hospital that long so he went back to the homeless camp.

Alocla ask him what kind of trouble did you get into day.

David took the pen out of his pocket and pull out the sim card and put it in the computer. If you watch you will see that I did not cause any trouble. It had recorded the whole time.

As Alocla watch the video. David took out his gun and took the clip out and the bullet in the chamber put the gun in the safe and pulled out another lock box and put the clip in it so to match the California gun laws.

So who is this girl Alocla asked?

Ammie and her sister live with us when they were taken away from their mother. All of us were already out of school. Mon and Dad just felt it was too quite so they help out and the two girls live with them till one graduated and the other went in the NAVY.

So how is this Ammie?

She is in the hospital now and will be for a few days. Are we staying here at the homeless camp till then?

No we will move closer to the hospital.

Good I don't like staying near this homeless camp. Look at all the trash. I didn't know a lot of these people that have diabetes half the people need shots and just leave the used needles just lay around.

Those are not for diabetes they are using it to take drugs of all kind.

Why would they take shots just for the heck of it? I didn't like when they gave us the shot after leaving aria 55.

Those were different kinds of shots those were for not catching some disease. The one they are taken is to get high, and feel happy,

Most of them take the shot and lay around and sleeping. I thought that is what it for now some just run around acting stupid, those are the ones I don't like and they scare me ,they are crazy, I thought they were like when you talking to your Guardian Angels. Talking to no one that only they can see.

David laughed it is a little thing, I think maybe they are.

They are not talking to their guardian Angles wish they were it would sure make it easier on us we could tell them when they are in trouble.

David heard but not Alocla. Well let's move from here to the hospital David said as he started securing things to move the motor home closer to the hospital.

What are you going to do with Ammie when she gets out of the hospital?

I have been trying to find her sister up in Washington. We will take her up there and she can watch out for her.

David and Alocla moved over to the hospital and the first night the hospital security cane by in the middle of the night asking why they were there when David explain about Ammie in the hospital the security went and check it out then came back said it was alright for one night but had to move tomorrow.

The next morning they check on Aimmie she was still incoherent so David started looking for a RV park close by but before they could.

Who should show but their friend form the

FBI but Mr. swan.

What the hell are you doing here David Asked?

The police department ran your plated on the jeep then again last night your bus.

So I thought I had better come out here and see what kind of trouble you had got in to this time.

Well come into my MOTOR HOME and I'll show you.

They went inside Swan look around this is kind a nice.

Yes I kind a grows on you sit down and watch the computer where David had down loaded everything on the sin card

After he had seen the whole thing MR. Swan look at David did you have to fire that damn gun, in the city limit. Can you make a copy of this in case I need it?

Yes but why would you need it Alocla asked. Did he do something wrong?

Yes, he didn't shoot the guys. Like I would have if I saw what they were doing.

David stuck in a stick drive and copy it then handed it to him.

Ok I'll talk with the hospital and get it clear for you to stay here in your Motor home as he looks around. Nice is all he said and walk out

CHAPTER 41

Buddy

Alocla and David were sitting around when an advertisement came on television about a Amtrak going from Seattle to New York. Alcoa's eyes lit up can we do that she asked?

Yes if that is what you want.

That does look like fun.

OK as David pick up his phone and makes the reservation. Putting down the phone we have seven days to get to Seattle. We will take the car and leave tomorrow. There was plenty of time so they put their motor home in storage. And took the jeep heading up toward the northwest they spent a day in Seattle seeing the sights then that night they put the jeep into storage and got on the train for a sightseeing trip across the United State seeing sights that you cannot see from any road.

They had a sleeping birth but spent most of the time up in the dome car. That is where they were. When the Log truck coming off a logging road that crosses the tracks in Montana. Hit the dome car, knocking it off the tracks and rolling it over on its side.

David was pinned under a table. He could see the mist of several Angels. He knew that appear when someone dies. Alocla, Alocla David called out, he receive no answered. Blue eyes are you out there?

She busy directing souls to the right path to heaven. It came from a voice David was sure he had heard before.

It came from the mist standing near him said.

Alocla how is she?

That is where, the one you call Blue eyes is directing Alocla she was one of her charges.

No No: she is alright.

I'm sorry to say she did not make it and is now in a better place. That is where the one you call blue eyes is at.

And who are you?

I'm your Guardian Angel.

What do I call you Shorty as David coughs a couple of times?

You always called me Buddy.

Hay that's the name I call my Teddy, David stopped there. Buddy turned up missing after the first truck wreck.

I know that's when you started getting the other ones, but I was giving the job of watching over you since I was doing it all along. Think back after Alaska you started hearing me, and you thought as everyone else that you were talking to yourself.

So why are you here now?

Because you are in bad shape and are not giving up If you just let me show you a better place.

But I'm not ready to give up yet.

I know: just like several times before. Only this time I don't think you are going to make it.

What about Blue eyes?

She is Alocla Guardian Angel she lead you to where Alocla was laying it wasn't her time yet. So if you will just follow me I will take you to her.

Sorry, I'm not ready; I still have a lot to do here and I don't want to travel down that road.

Printed in the USA
CPSIA information can be obtained
at www.ICGtesting.com
JSHW021224011023
49140JS00001B/9